CREATIVE OBSESSION

SECOND EDITION

CREATIVE
Obsession

Philosophic Life in Broad Daylight

AN APOMARY

VIATOR E. O'LEVITER

TEMESCAL
PUBLISHING

To the blazing artists and epic travelers,
on a one-way ticket, who will forge new worlds.

SYNOPSIS

Creative Obsession is an *apomary*, a fragmented fusion of *aphorisms*, *apothegms* and *apologues*, which depicts a "boiling pot" of philosophy with astonishing succinctness.

The fervent protagonist of *Creative Obsession* is Homer Dogg, "a hardcore traveler, an honest scholar, and an infatuated artist." The apomary spans Homer Dogg's fleeting, peripatetic life, while unearthing a deep-rooted connectedness of *aesthetic*, *epistemic*, and *ethic* thinking. *Creative Obsession* celebrates "creative people of all stripes, who live and work passionately, resiliently, and with their eyes wide open." It portrays *philosophic life in broad daylight* for the "firstborn of the Third Millennium."

"Homer Dogg says in ten sentences (sometimes less) what others don't say in a whole book."
—F. W. Nietzsche

"A literary, aporistic and, if you ask me, successful experiment in harnessing the omnipresent powers of abductive logic."
—C. S. Peirce

In just fifty-six eclectic segments (and a revealing afterword), *Creative Obsession* presents a glistening mosaic of a wide-open, un-universal, *neo-philosophic* landscape.

Viator E. O'Leviter is from Oakland, California.

CONTENTS

Afterword

CREATIVE OBSESSION

PRELUDE

Phenomenal success, truckloads of cash, and hundreds of very close friends are nice things to have, and so naturally, we want them desperately. But what most people *really* want, if not the obvious trappings, is to have interesting, *positively fascinating* lives. A penniless man (in an old fable) will be perfectly content, provided he does not suffer from a cold and boring existence, while a rich man will be miserable to the end, if he can no longer stand the muddled routines of his predictable life.

We humans are a frantic lot — absolutely, wholeheartedly crazy to have interesting lives. In childhood and beyond, year after year, we strive to experience the most astonishing, enthralling events. So, what stops us? Why do we, time and again, lose pleasure in what we are becoming? Why do so many irrepressible souls grow so amazingly decrepit?

The problem, I think, is that we succumb to our fears. We feel it in our bones that an interesting life is a dangerous desire. Life's imposing fascination and dire endeavors, this *imperative to adapt* is the very meaning of risk, where grievous injury and abrupt endings are rife. Also, to the extent we remain unimpressed by the grinding habits and faceless regularity of civilized life, we become less disposable and poorly disposed to various enterprises — and so in *natural* worlds, where scarcity is as predictable as the extinction of species, we bow to the dismally doubling toil and increasingly volatile, *economic* troubles at hand. Lastly, we tremble like lost kittens, while the *blessings of community* appear more distant and less assuring, should we venture "outside the box," and there may be extra piles of ridicule and irritating indignities to deal with. The chance of becoming a genuine oddball (a lonely eccentric, a pathetic apostate) is much greater, whenever someone seeks to command his or her own destiny.

It's the job of preachers and pundits to remind us of our fears as often as possible. This may seem meddlesome and intrusive, but instead, let's take it for what it is — a fair warning. Still, our loftiest aspirations (these primordial desires) remain unaffected. We will engage life fervidly, in a first and last embrace. We will build and cultivate interesting, cherished lives, as far as our abilities, learning, and good fortune should allow. We propose to examine this existence intensely, and then even *more* intensely, come what may.

Such a deliberate and torrid engagement exemplifies the *philosophic* life. It favors clarity of thought, courage of choice, and a circumspect knowledge. All of this is interrelated. And so in philosophy, as in life, there evolves theories of meaning, methodologies and conceptions of reality — a seamless web, woven over the millennia from the common threads of human experience. It offers us a noble, perilous ethic, where one's own existence might become one's own creative obsession.

• • •

Dear reader, the "apomary" is a *literary mosaic* of assorted, *aphoristic fragments* pieced and puzzled into pixelated, *"aporistic" pictures*. It lays out densely layered, brief segments in a meticulously reduced concoction of theme, tense, mood, metaphor, and grammatical person, forming webs of characters, settings, and events that congeal into dynamic dioramas of the mind, like the solidifying dots of a realistic wirephoto, or the haunting images of a pointillistic masterpiece (the fine details of a linear language transfigured into spheres of crystalized understanding).

The apomary's conjoining aphorisms, apothegms, and apologues (the spiraling abstracts, epigrams, and parables) suffuse and illuminate an abiding plot that's not too hard to get, especially if you like to indulge occasionally in well-chewed and mulled-over, blissful bouts of reading. The story is about creative people of all stripes, who live and work passionately, resiliently, and with their eyes wide open. It is a *saga of humanity*, a tale of the undaunted, living soul of a distressed species, which I've told in as few words and with all the depiction I could handle. Under the circumstances, the Afterword must serve as my intrinsically incomplete-able and, if I may, respectfully submitted explanation.

The protagonist and narrator of *Creative Obsession* (this metamorphic memoir and not-so-massive missive) is Homer Dogg — a hardcore traveler, an honest scholar, and an infatuated artist. His character is an admixture, as his name suggests, of two broadly representative personas from Greek antiquity. The first, of course, is Homer, the blind poet, the artist who gave us Odysseus and Hector. The second is Diogenes, a.k.a. "the Dog," the greatest bohemian perhaps there ever was, the godfather of all virtuously declared and openly waged counterculture.

— VEO

APHORISMS, APOTHEGMS,
AND APOLOGUES

THE CLIMBER

One morning the climber set out alone to scale the highest mountain in the land. All his life, he wished for little else, and now, finally, he was well prepared. But he told no one he would make the attempt, not ever, not a word. The climb was treacherous and brutal, as the climber knew it would surely be. He scaled the forbidding and unforgiving escarpments, into the face of a screaming, freezing wind. The long ascent tested every ounce of his patience, strength, and courage, and with each step the world around him and below him loomed larger and more spectacular.

At last, he set foot atop the towering, high palisade. It was the consummate moment, a flourishing climax of heart-pounding magnificence and *over-whelming* satisfaction. The climber had seen, and there would be no doubt in his mind, that this was his great achievement. He stood tall upon the icy, precarious peak. He stretched his arms out wide, he threw back his head and delivered, into a vast and empty sky, the *resounding*, ecstatic cries of a knowing soul and uncompromised spirit.

But it was not a good day to die, and so, after a few minutes, the climber regained his composure. He took a last look around and then, with a sigh, he began his slow, careful descent back to the village.

The climber returned late at night. The people didn't even know he'd been gone. Years later, he drew an exquisite map *but told no one* what was waiting, not ever, not a word. He wanted it that way, and so it was. Until the end, the climber remained steadfast, ever faithful to his life and deed. He had been to the mountain by fair means, leaving no trace, because it was there.

ACIDHEAD

How embarrassing when I catch myself believing that I know the truth of my faith. Just like some fully functioning fanatic, I think in terms of "belief," "knowledge," "truth," and "faith," all at the same time (white noise of the brain), and the gods appear again before me, like doting slaves and magic elves. Once again, I have mistaken a moment of extreme confusion for a moment of crystal clarity. It happens all the time, this wishful thinking.

PEDANTRY

When we were little, someone kept telling us, "There are precisely *five* senses. Seeing, hearing, smelling, tasting, and feeling!" We were so sweet. We believed it! Every syllable. (A few ambitious youngsters even memorized that stuff.)

Later on, the vanguard moved in, and now we have precisely *six* senses. (The key to a higher awareness, these serious wits insisted, was to stick a different name or number on the thing.)

As for us, we are recovering, inch by inch, from our rote reasoning and boorish learning, perhaps feeling exasperated and *thoroughly* dissatisfied. We are constrained to work out and overcome the myths, prejudices, and *pedantry* we absorbed so completely during those lost, fantastical years.

CLAIRVOYANT

Then I remember when all the kids, hanging out after school, would try to imagine that super-dictions were real. You know, things like extra-wet water, extra-round circles, extra-zoological animals — whatever. It was just a game. No honest and sane child would ever *truly* believe that super-dictions were real.

The coolest super-dictions would usually have some twisted language. Like, *extra-sensory perception*. Not a very sensible combination of words, when you think about it. But turn it on its head, twist it back the other way and consider, or simply ask yourself, have you ever experienced *extra-perceptive sensation*? You probably have! All the time.

Sometimes (maybe you've also had this experience) extra-perceptive sensation can become extra-strange and terribly, horribly sensational. Should we ponder, therefore, the existence of the *supernatural*? That'd be easy enough, if words gave off their own light. But isn't the "supernatural" just another extravagant super-diction? (Within a single word!)

This kind of thinking can make me start to feel uneasy. If I'm living in the midst of an increasingly strange, yet profoundly *un*-supernatural reality, do I risk my vital, deeply embedded belief in the natural? Answer: Some of the time, sure. And sure, existence is scary. But why, during my brief encounter with an awesome universe, should I use trending words and ornate utterances (such as, "supernatural") like a tranquilizer? Why should I *sedate* my senses at the shiny shrines of a prior, synthetic knowledge, or upon the solid ground of a fancy terminology? Somebody, wake me up! Am I such a shivering, stupefied creature in the presence of a dark mystery, that I must first always seize the latest or the greatest off-the-shelf explanation, and then *delude* myself that I am a great lover of knowledge, when quite the contrary, I am merely a great fornicator, vulgar and promiscuous, getting humped along the way by so many shoddy descriptions and empty narratives, one more right after another . . . (Then I'd hear, "What are you, crazy? It's a *game*, Homer!")

KNOT FAIR

Ladies and Gentlemen of the jury:

In the Old West, the Bad Guys were usually hung. But judges were hard to impress in them days, so the Bad Guys were usually hanged. It served them boys rite. It is a capitol offense to deliberately and maliciously split an English infinitive. All them nameless, no-good modifiers needed . . . dangling, mercilessly!

It is therefore *indescribably* clear, because since that which, moreover, pertains to no man is *absolutely* certain. (Naturally. *But of course.* As it were.)

And in final conclusion, we shall indubitably experience, lest it be known, all that we might see. And if I can briefly summarize at the present time, allow me permission — no, permit me the *allowance* to once again most positively ensure you that, irregardless, this is not fare!

COINCIDENTAL
COSMOS

I was crashing this wild party in L.A., and I got into a conversation with a stunning, sultry woman wearing a black, slinky dress and about three pounds of quartz and silver jewelry. It turns out she's a psychic. I mean, the way she was dressed, I guess I read her mind about her being a psychic — or maybe she just told me. Anyway, everything was proceeding very nicely, thank you, when she decided to announce that it wasn't a "coincidence" we had met. She told me, in her low and mysterious tone of voice, that there were no coincidences within the cosmic plane. And so I, like a flipped-out, postmodern motor-head, instead of pretending I was impressed, I had to tell her that, on the contrary, *everything* out there was a *totally* random, virtually *perfect* coincidence, that at rock bottom, the sun rising in the east, and even two plus two equaling four, were stuck in some contingent kind of cosmic coincidence, that only this morning, the odds of us meeting and sleeping together that night was a seventy-three trillion-to-one shot and hey, would she like to beat the odds? (Oh yeah. I nailed it.) After a couple of seconds though, she said I was *right* — that it *was* a seventy-three trillion-to-one shot, and then she walked away.

BORN AGAIN

We spent half the day flirting and half the night making love, and so as always, I managed to convince myself that I was madly smitten, *positively* head over heels, or worse. Then she turned to me and said, "I am *so* certain that in a previous life you were . . . a Comanche warrior. Were you? I know it . . . I can *feel* it."

Wow! Was it because of my spear? My second reaction was to wonder if Comanche women had any unusual fetishes that I should know about. Then I felt weirdly disillusioned at the thought of maybe, just having had great sex with a corseted fashionista, when it was her vivacious, free spirit that had made her so especially attractive in the first place. Anyway, she was expecting a reply. So I told her, as candidly as I could, "Sorry, Beautiful. I'm no Comanche. I . . . was born once. Guess I'll die once, too."

It struck me that she was startled by my answer. But of course she kept her cool. Then she spilled her guts: "Well, my belief system is metaphysical, and it . . . requires an open mind. Many of us are destined to have several lives. In fact, there's quite a lot of corresponding, scientific proof about past life . . . regressions and out-of-the-body experiences."

For once in my life, I managed to keep my mouth shut. She seemed disappointed that we weren't going to indulge in an exchange of flattering fish tales from our illustrious past lives. As we shared the awkward moment, still catching our breath, she snuggled close and whispered, ever so reassuringly, "But of *course*, you *do* believe . . . in life beyond the mundane material realities, in the *true* meaning of truth in a . . . life *beyond* life, right?"

You know, winding down after a passionate splurge of sweaty abandon and rapturous, ravenous coitus is an ideal time for openness and honesty, and I sincerely wanted to learn something honest about this intriguing and alluring woman (although I really *do* wish she had changed the subject). I kissed her breast, then I gazed into those deep, green eyes and whispered back, "You mean, do I believe . . . in life *after* death? Actually, I'm still trying to get a handle on this predicament of death, after life . . . Do *you* believe in death after life?"

That was a mistake. It's one thing to fiddle with somebody's spirituality *du jour*, quite another to burrow into the pillars of an excitable, monocratic psyche. She rose with the usual, amazing grace, and she stared far-off, into the infinitesimal reaches of space. Then she spoke, with impressive, indignant incredulity, "Homer, are you an *a*-theist?"

. . . Huh? Now what kind of a question is that to ask a defenseless, naked ape? More often than not, it's rude and ridiculous to talk religion when you're in bed with someone you might not understand. (I keep forgetting that.) But no matter — I had to think of an apology fast. She was buttoning up and fading away. I was losing her, I could *feel* it.

PASSION'S PASSAGE

Through it all, you're back on the road at the edge of the world, traversing an endlessly edgeless globe—fervently resolved to know what it's like. You *need* the earthy people, the hidden byways, and distant horizons, *desiring without end*, to understand how it feels (how *everything* feels), taking your turn, seeing it all, *not missing your chance*, ever.

It's hard, sometimes, so what. For you it's all a gift, another breath of life, more free air! You crave the unsettling possibilities. You want this to be perfect, to be brilliant, awesome, unbelievable, and then, to get away again, to overcome, *and to recover*, maintaining your desire and once more, regaining the edge. Always another venture, a different place to be. A new city, a strange country, one more *unimaginable* landscape. You know that someday you'll stop, and then, your story is over — it's the next-to-the-last chapter, *the book is closing* — time spins faster, and *you're waiting for nothingness*! No! Don't stop! Not you. No way.

NO EXIT

Suppose you realized suddenly that you were buried inside a small, dark vault under a 200-foot mudslide. You have maybe a six or an eight-hour air supply, assuming the walls of the vault don't cave-in first. In no uncertain terms, there is absolutely no hope for getting out alive. An unseen, unstoppable clock begins ticking away the last minutes and hours of your life.

Now cast your fate. You have two choices: (1) Remain calm, and then die. (2) Do something, and then die.

The first choice defers the unpleasantries. It ensures tranquility, and it upholds precious dignities. Who would reproach our sisters and brothers, who in the throes of grief and mortal terror, seek a path to inner peace? Who would wish to disprove another person's quiet prayer for eternal salvation? The first choice engenders the great religious and mystic movements.

It was the monumental choice of Orpheus, Ezekiel, Philo, and Paul. It is the vision and choice made possible through faith, hope, and blessed mercy.

But whenever these timeless qualities have been nurtured and transfigured, under our most primordial affections, into a semblance of wisdom, courage, and love, a vision of the vault becomes a commandment to act. A sublime imperative comes into effect — it is a *perversion* to squander away the last hours. It is a grotesque waste to disregard the inevitable, fleeting choices which unfold during life. We confront voracious, world-effacing desires for ever more engaging and enduring work. We are shaken from our hallucinations and stupors by life's acute limitation, with the understanding that a person lives and thrives, or does not, through all that is perceived and created, and in the end, by what got done.

What will you *do* then, down in the vault? . . . Start digging — what the hell. Scratch an epitaph into the wall. Tremble and laugh . . .

PERFECT MINDS

Imagine a cosmos as trifling and as limited as your imagination. Would you feel any better? Here's another one: Imagine the sphere of potential human understanding appearing like a tiny, fragile bubble in a boundless ocean of unknowable possibilities.

Sure enough, in order to harmonize human experience with human understanding, it might be much easier to fashion the human experience into a dull, repetitive and paltry affair. Someone could spend half his life, for example, sitting in a cave, contemplating his navel, or exploring the vast and untracked spaces between his ears. Then one amazing day (maybe longer) . . . *Eureka! Wisdom!* Or perhaps not.

Is there an alternative to the *eternalistic* sense of perfection? Could the human experience withstand a perfectly *disharmonious*, radical opposition to the cosmos? Is "the law of nature" a perfect contradiction in terms?

THE MEASURE OF
ALL THINGS

The remarkable beauty of the Earth is not a compelling reason for the existence of anything. What's so beautiful out there is not *nature*, but rather humankind's life-enabling faith in a timeless congruence of the rational mind and the natural world — this primal, aesthetic *reaction* to our peculiar knowledge of being. Mother Nature does not think of herself as being beautiful. How silly! (How absurd.)

It is our nonsensical habit to award the badge of reality to the most vague of ideals, such as our ancient belief in the existence of "beauty," while we often idealize perfectly discrete, nuanced objects with our rampant abuse of high-sounding, catch-all nouns, like when we lump all the hard rocks and oceans of the world into some Never-Never Land called "nature."

The Beauty of Nature can be a mind-smothering realization. Be guarded in your thinking, if you become mesmerized by the radiance of a spectacular sunset. Remember, man may not be the measure of all things, but he *is* the measure of all gods.

PATHOLOGICAL MAN

What!? The soul is *immortal*? And only the *body* dies? But did you ever meet a human being who had no soul? Did you catch that ominous, detached look in the liar's eye, just as he started to smile? (Or did you ever stop to consider why it is that suicide is so common?)

Even in our own, mad scramble to secure a permanent faith and tame the universe, there comes a time when our soul — our essential being (this very rarified *knowing*), our mind, reason, conscience and consciousness — becomes the time-worn, type-cast obstacle to every easy explanation and convenient revelation. It twists and deforms itself into a mere irritant, a meager vexation of the desires.

And yet how *easy* it is, in these convoluted moments, to overcome the soul! How easy it is, if we are careless, utterly to destroy the soul.

HOME RUN

It happened that a prudent man was alone in his hotel room, at the end of a routine business trip, when he fell into a fitful sleep.

He had an extremely realistic dream. He was at Yankee Stadium, but he was in uniform! He had finally made it to the majors! Not only that, the manager had just called on him to pinch-hit with the bases loaded, the game was on the line, and the crowd was going wild!

As the prudent man was selecting his bat — finding one that would look splendid, but wasn't too heavy — the manager came over to him. "Listen up, Kid," said the manager. "This game is different. There's no balls and no strikes. You get to play in just one game. You're getting just one at-bat, and you get just *one* pitch. You got that?"

The prudent man nodded, but he was distracted by the cheering crowd. He felt immensely important as he stepped-up to the plate. The fearsome pitcher tried to stare him down, but the prudent man would *certainly not* look him in the eye. Then the pitcher delivered a scorching fastball, which looked a little high and maybe just a bit outside, so the prudent man didn't swing. (He just stood there, prudently.)

"Yerrrrr OUT!" shouted the umpire, and the crowd went stone-cold silent. Then the manager motioned the prudent man toward the showers. "That's it, Kid," he said. "You're through."

The prudent man jolted up. He was shaking, hyperventilating — in a suffocating panic. "I shall *never* have this horrible nightmare, *ever again!*" said the prudent man to himself, alone in his hotel room.

And in fact, he did not have this nightmare again, until a couple of years later, when the doctors told him that the tumor in his brain was a hopeless case. After that, for the last days of his life, the prudent man had this same nightmare whenever he fell asleep, and it became more terrifying to him each time.

MORAL TEMPERAMENT

A mark of moral temperament: to be ashamed of one's fear. A mark of feeble souls: to indulge fear, thus to avoid shame.

THE RULE OF LAW

Those who will only dream of Peace on Earth are the innocent devotees of death. Peace is a towering, abstract idea that relates to the absence of war — it sure as Hell on Earth isn't the other way around. The coteries of peace foreshadow the closeted war-worshiper, as each black-gutted annihilation (yet another tsunami of death-by-meat-grinder) grows so conveniently abhorrent. It warms the cynic's pale, thin blood. It lends moral authority to cowards and provides a conviction for the meek.

We shall rest upon sweet, eternal dreams of Peace on Earth. Or we recognize the greater challenge and the greater hope — we seek to change the rules of war.

MERRY-GO-ROUND

The pen is mightier than the sword . . .

Certainly! Indubitably! And what of it? *Money* is mightier than the pen. Fortunately, knowledge is mightier than money. (Thank goodness.) But knowledge — unfortunately, the sword is mightier than knowledge — and so it goes.

My *personal* advice? Avoid the system. My counsel? Be damned well prepared *before* you cross it.

HERO WORSHIP

Every lie, blasphemy, snafu, error, and false assumption ever devised by human beings started out as something that was supposed to be true to somebody.

The Goddess of Truth is a poor and eternally abused creature. She is covered in mud, battered and bleeding. Yet once again we will dress her up, unwashed, in new shining armor, then throw her back down into the pit and imagine she's up on some magnificent pedestal, resplendent and invulnerable.

THE SEDUCERS

The world is chock-full of crybabies and bellyachers — people who, deep down inside, want revenge. They will use the most subtle persuasion they can think of to get you to hate what they hate. Or else, if you just laugh, they will wish you were miserable. Or better still, dead. Be careful. Some of these nice folks are smart. They will gather in groups and say things like, "Join us! Be one with us! Together we shall *destroy* this wickedness, and our names will live *forever*!"

DON JUAN

Carlos Castaneda is a great deceiver. He freely admits this, if you have learned to "see." This master of allegory shuns the aesthetics of mind. He disavows imperatives and constraints born of piety, fortitude, counsel and understanding, and his disciples do not see the allegory. They cannot conceive that deception is the base confession of his philosophy. "Behold the unreality!" he tantalizes plying supplicants. "Be the foolish sorcerer's apprentice, and I will die laughing."

THE PHILOSOPHER KING

I was exhausted. Somehow, I managed to drag myself to the top of the last ridge. I had walked all day, and in twilight, then into the night, I think . . . I'm not sure anymore.

Before me, the soaring, first rays of dawn were piercing the jagged divide. Below me and about a half-mile beyond was my destination, the old man's shack. It was difficult, in the gathering light, to make out his shack from the windswept desolation. I shuddered at the sight of that stark, foreboding landscape. "Oh no, this *couldn't* be a nightmare," I thought as I peered downward. "I am too cold to be asleep. I am really here! This *must* be real."

I had visited the old man many times before. Sometimes he would interrogate me rudely for hours. Other times he would say nothing. He was powerful and arrogant. I resented his unyielding self-assurance and his keen, penetrating understanding. I truly envied the depth of his experience and his unapproachable, extraordinary intimacy with the Earth. Oh yes, I *loathed* his inscrutable ways — I hated *all* of this! And I feared the dog. You must believe me, I never wanted to change.

I started down from the ridge, and I soon realized the old man was sitting on his porch. He was waiting for me, I had no doubt of that. He sat cross-legged, arms folded, and stonelike against the post. I had seen him sitting this way before. But as I came closer, I noticed a strange, disturbing difference. Something was wrong with the old man. His body was slack, and his head was cocked to one side. Nervously I continued on, even more slowly than before. Then, when I was only a few feet away, a shadow crept from his face, and the old man was in clear view. I gagged, and I staggered back. A foul dread washed over me — the old man was dead!

His mouth was agape, and a blackened, twisted tongue stuck against his lower lip. Large flies swarmed all around him. His eyes were fixed in an upward stare, they bulged and oozed grotesquely. It was hideous. My heart was beating wildly, as I stepped onto the porch. Nausea curdled my stomach, as I placed my hand upon his shoulder, and I gazed into that hoary, dead face. Guardedly, mindfully, I sat down beside him, unable to avert my eyes. For a long moment, I sat there staring, sickened, horrified, and utterly fascinated. Then, assuaged by a tranquil sunrise, and for no good reason, I felt for a pulse along the side of his neck.

Just then it happened, if indeed, it could have happened. In an instant, his unfettered corpse pivoted toward me, and his vise-like hands fastened to my upper arms. His face was in a sudden, terrible rage. I convulsed, and my heart seized as he lifted my body while his eyes, now blazing and fierce, tore through me — his jaw dropped, and a shrill, hellish shriek filled my ears, that maniacal sound distorting weirdly into head-splitting screams before I realized that somehow, it was I who was screaming. Helpless and in terror I collapsed, and the world around me began to dissolve . . .

Looking up, I found that I was sprawled on my belly, a couple hundred yards from the shack. Perhaps a few minutes had passed. Perhaps another day. I just don't know. My mouth tasted like dust and puke, and the old man was crouched over me. He was laughing at me, again. He knew, I would come back.

BEAT

The road can crush me, someday it will. I mean, *nothing* will harm me, except like, underestimating the familiar or like, overlooking the strange. So keep me moving. I'm still breathing. Man, what's coming? I got to make it. Damn me, I got to know.

PERIPATETIC

When you travel light, you make your own luck. You sleep where you are, and you eat what there is.

Travel achieves credibility. It earns the right to teach . . . *Hard travel!* (You will teach hard things.)

SUBVERSIVE INTENT

The wanderer is a subversive. Although, if he lived in another time and place, for example, during protracted religious wars, while multitudes cry hysterically and incessantly for their salvation, then the wanderer would not subvert. He would assume an ideal, hold it inviolable, and build from it a calming repertoire of agreeable teachings. He would heal, explain, soothe, and deliver.

But in a complacent world, where the war of independence has become the war of domination, where religion succumbs to politics, and science is warped by sycophants and greed, the wanderer rises with an unbridled passion to lay humanity bare against the wind, a rootless thinker obsessed by the discovery of life on Earth, indifferent to convention, oblivious to the transitory corruption of morals.

BRAIN RUST

On a steaming, tropical island, in a stinking, broken-down hotel, in my dingy little room, lying on this damp, decaying mattress. Breathing stale air trapped inside this filthy mosquito net. Mixing iodine and whisky into my water (the sugar's gone). Gecko shit covers everything, no wind, no rain for days, insects flying, crawling everywhere (nothing else moves). No water for the toilet, my food's going bad, I got cramps all over my guts . . . I'm getting nervous, dengue and dysentery, festering through the mangroves, creeping into my skin. Boat didn't come this week. Maybe next week. Can't sleep, can't breathe. Can't even think.

HELL'S BELLS

I am defeated by my own weakness. I am devoid of inspiration, even to get up from this chair. I am tortured by thoughts of undone duties and lost expectations, my mind is mired in oppressive images of failures and broken promises. Cruel memory! Unfaithful, revolting world! Revolting me! Me, drowning in wretched self-pity. Gasping, struggling once again for the last wisp and scent of spent dreams.

WORLDWISE

Do what it takes to raise the odds that absolutely amazing and incredible things will happen in your life. Nurture your sense of astonishment. Nurture your sense of humor. Nurture your sense of reason. And so, do not deceive.

Live slowly. Savor the magnificence of an ephemeral existence. Get as much raw, uncensored experience into your life as you can. Get as many lives into your life as possible, and be enthralled by the *simultaneities* of a living mind. (Know that past and future lives are the phantasms of frolicking children, anguished souls, and those who will be bored unto death.)

THE OUTER LIMITS

In a temporal universe, we can only assimilate the past, intuit the present, and deduce the future.

Our knowledge and faith, no matter how certain, will not survive the last human mind. The cosmos does not need our permission to exist. The mountain doesn't care. The climber is truly alone.

THE INTERLUDE

This is a good time to remind ourselves of Nietzsche's astute observation that "genius" is ordinary, but "spirit" is very rare.

THE ALTAR OF PYTHAGORAS

Of all the things we care about in life, we value most of all the consummate certainty of mathematical knowledge. Even as children, we were keenly aware of the inherent supremacy of mathematics. Its *fabulously* analytic properties and deductive, stepwise method were clearly the measure of every other science. That demonstrative abstractness and robust "non-actuality" had fathered such *precise* equations, and if nothing else, we learned to respect this mysterious chariot of Absolute Knowledge, this indispensable linchpin of the universe.

Real mathematicians lead lives of uncommon mental toil. In return, they enjoy an unequaled vision of rational perfection. Mathematicians are transfixed by the most glittering revelations of star-studded genius. They bask in an assortment of refined, matho-mystical, transcendental trips. Their obsession and inspiration is constantly revitalized as piece by piece, before their eyes, the greatest puzzle in creation is set firmly into place. (The laws *enshrined*. Numbers made flesh! The ordination of ordinals, the *deification* of formulae!) But they are also human, and in the end, the obsession wears thin, and the rewards dissolve like nullities into empty sets. It follows that mathematicians *never* perfect the art.

HARD SCIENCE

Oddly enough, the Great Mathematician perfected the art. Although at first, when he was finishing school, he was beginning to believe that he had fully mortgaged his faith in figures. Then he experienced a supreme moment of mathematical creation.

Actually, he had just been in a bar fight the day before, and he was sitting in his boyfriend's hot tub, nursing a fat lip. Suddenly, without warning, while mindlessly contemplating the bubbles in his beer, he was engulfed by a staggering, whirling host of *astoundingly* unconstrainable conceptions, unleashed by as many elusive leaps of shimmering, irrepressible intellect, those bright, billowing particles yet forming strange and crystalline apparitions! All through the evening and into the night, the Great Mathematician endured a relentless, full-scale eruption of a luxuriant, tumultuous, and fantastically focused creativity — *ecstatically*, and from out of a beer bubble, his scrupulous, incisive insight transposed transfiguring torrents of realigning relations and ethereal impressions (barely intelligible, and still *ingeniously* cohesive), blazing an unbroken path to the ends of his most presumptuous, *outrageous* supposition: the mathematically mystifying Next Step! (A somewhat level-headed youth, he never would have anticipated such a brain-twisting, life-wrenching epiphany, although perhaps, within the shrouded chambers of his unconscious obsessions, he had prepared boldly, fervently, *incessantly* for this monumental breakthrough.) Throughout that flickering night, and until the dawn enticed him to sleep, the Great Mathematician embraced the hallowed splendor of a life devoted to lofty learning — an exacting scholar, naked and wet, and courting the irreversibly ridiculous, was abruptly consecrated by a *very* close encounter, by an unadulterated, uncontainable catharsis of lucid, frenetic imagery and *sustained abduction*. He brought to the airy, supersensible regions of his thrashed and churning head, from the dusty remnants of a thousand lost dreams, a once inconceivable *a priori*, an *immutable* realization, a radically original distillation of a mind-altering, world-shattering, more perfect method and genesis of analysis!

As soon as he woke up, the Great Mathematician set out to systematize and formalize his preposterously timeless, pristine creation. Greatly inspired by the clarity and scope of his vision, he worked tirelessly, day and night, with unmatched professional dedication and with prodigious, distinguished skill. He sweated blood, lost his job, and completed his masterpiece in scarcely thirteen years — his mind's work impeccably put upon paper, expressed in the unassailable, universal language of mathematics.

When it was time to publish this revolutionary work, the Great Mathematician almost hesitated. With sadness and pride, however, he sent his sublime brainchild out into the world, his inner knowledge given up to science, dedicated forever to the common heritage of humankind. The Great Mathematician sorely missed his life's inspiration.

The publication *instantly* set off fireworks *galore*! It made lots of money and secured lasting fame for the Great Mathematician. The top-dog mathematicians fell all over themselves, declaring that he was an exalted, Grand Poobah-in-waiting. But of course, they didn't know, nor would the duly assembled fellows have cared (as dedicated specialists) about the immeasurable, resplendent outburst of mathematical knowledge, which took place that night in the hot tub. They praised him, as well they should have, for his exquisitely crafted formulations. They admired the elegant simplicity of his demonstrations, applauding with relief and delight as they recognized the ancient axioms and eternalistic theorems of mathematics lurking beneath the insurgent ideas. They reveled in their ability to comprehend this bedazzling, new paradigm of proof, *flattered* to confirm its validity (a self-levitating certainty!) for themselves and for all time. Once again, the Mighty Electors declared, the preeminence of mathematics was on display. Once again, it was opportune to scoff at all the "soft" sciences.

The Great Mathematician drew back from the accolades, and he canceled the European tour. He had come to believe that mathematics was no longer merely hard science. He could only conclude that his precious work, if not the entire body of mathematical knowledge, perhaps *all* knowledge began as a strikingly stable, transgressive hypothesis (an *organic* process, conceived *necessarily* in pure synthesis), a palpable premonition of intra-phenomenal realities; in short, an unmediated, synergistic conflation of effect and idea (the very essence of mind) that no mathematical form of equivalence could even begin to assimilate. And still, it must be assimilated! This outlandish, vital process was surely the wellspring of his science, his beloved mathematics! The Great Mathematician was impatient for another supreme moment of creation. Within weeks, his frustration had ripened into a feverish desperation.

The Great Mathematician began to think: These unremitting memories of streaming sensations, these neuro-coursing, arcing exabytes of data each day, were at each moment of life subjected to the unyielding mechanisms of psyche, logic, faith, and then by some *further*, immensely complex process, this inscrutable soup would be precipitously and involuntarily, consciously and unconsciously chopped, dissected, blended, and re-conglomerated into original knowledge (or conceivably, into original delusions) of *probabilistic* extrusions from a *dimensionless* reality, shaped by discoverable, heritable, and not-so-*a-priori* aesthetics, the *describably* transcendent, hypothetically systemic substance of *something-being-known*, which informs the soul and reveals the engine of *creative* human thought, and ultimately of *all* thought, or at least of *his* thought, and *this*, of all the physiology, phenomena, and intension of mind upon cosmos, could *not even supposedly* be random — already, by means of the most brilliantly refined, abductive modes of contemplation, as yet untouched by science, this process *could* be indistinctly observable, imprecisely controllable and inexplicitly predictable, and *that* was what the Great Mathematician had to believe.

WHY IS THIS?

The nature of your intellect is not determined by the answers you accept, but by the questions you ask.

SCARY PLANET

Out of sheer chaos, the first idea is universal Order. For centuries, our teachers and high priests have observed the unchanging stars. They have drawn circles into the sand and have dreamed of the boundless knowledge which lay within their grasp.

The second idea is cosmic Un-Order. Above us, surpassing the heavens, beyond the hundred billions of bright, predictable galaxies (eternally inconceivable, and inexpressible parsecs past *any* observation or cogent concept of analysis), *one thousand trillion edgeless universes*, unorientable, one-sided planes of reality — *exotic existences*, embracing ten thousand trillion physicalistic symmetries enveloping the undulating waves and mixing folds of *discrete* dimensions of time — expand, collapse, bounce around and collide, like so many molecules in a hot balloon. Yet even this bottomless cauldron of universes is an event of complete insignificance across a continuum of ten thousand quadrillion distinct cauldrons, a radiating infinitude fully subsumed in the infinite, infinitely twisting storms of *raging continua* streaking randomly within and throughout evanescent, meta-dimensional ethers clustering by further billions of trillions, like teeming effusions into spiraling quanta, cascading transiliently, forming further, fluidic fields of fusing, super-plasmic particles ever-condensing unto über-cosmic, ultra-encompassing clouds of extra-un-enumerable proto-realities *and beyond*, and . . . do you want this to be finite? Is it all "*One*?" (Do we have any *choice* in the matter?)

Even now, within this minuscule speck of a uni-verse, we are encountering space, time, matter, and energy on a scale, both large and small, already stuff-ing the limits of human conceivability. Our visions are becoming unworthy of our mathematics. (Or is it the other way around?) There is a lot of catching-up to do.

So why must we envision that certainty and truth go hand in hand? Science has become quite com-fortable with the understanding that "truth" conveys poetic meaning to the least disorganized, realistic apprehension of the most expedient, probable expla-nation of events. Science implicitly provides that only wholesale, protolinguistic generalities in the mind, like those of light, color, shape, name, and number, could render nature discernible, identifiable, and reasonably fixed. Once again, *science* has led the way — and metaphysics must follow. The infallible philodox and the armchair philosopher have every right to be embarrassed by the progress of science. Their stock-in-trade, those rock-solid demonstrations of Truth, the *emanations* of an everlasting Order (for a perfectly reflected Reality) are beginning to appear like half-baked, adolescent fantasies.

Perhaps the emanations of Order are nothing less than humanity's genius-fueled *abstractions* out of a supposed *Un-Order* (no less than our superbly human hypotheses, steeped in *very* intricately evolved, neural-temporal fabrics), from the minutest of essences and immensurate totality of an unspeakable reality and *un*-singular cosmos — transcending representation, obliterating orientation, and *devoid* of correspondence — from the crushing depths of an incomprehensible, timeless, *dimensionless* abyss.

Since the dawn of human reasoning, we have scrambled like bugs on a hot skillet to "discover" (factualize), out of primal formlessness, events of the world or events of the mind having various recurrences, correlations, and waves of probability. These assimilations, when given a sublime coloring, have served and will always serve as "the Truth." And since this beginning, the unshakable faith of peoples and nations notwithstanding, the Truth has never stopped changing.

Meanwhile, within "the Un-Order," first the appearance of things, and then language, law, logic, and consciousness itself have become known to us as metaphors, assimilates in themselves and harbingers of an unprepossessed, pragmatic paradigm — these *life-enabling*, flourishing filtrates of the brain, a glimmer of grammar embedded beneath a roiling mash of exceedingly unimaginable, exo-universal propensities and uncountably infinite, complementary modes of existence and equivalence.

The postulation of a dimensionless Un-Order, however remote, however close to us, is inescapable. Through these incipient intuitions of an all-too-human, universal law, and by the inexorably un-objective reality of quantum mechanics — and then (good heavens), from the *extra-dimensional* domains of semi-substantive superstrings (un-affected by weightless theorems) — the *intellect* of humankind shall also, alas, be firmly cast out of Eden. In worlds of unrelenting change and interminable refinement, there are no more miracles, no gods worth remembering.

Variation incites the inference of existence, fomenting facts grossly exposed to the ineffable geometries of an incognizable cosmos. We experience, irreconcilably, an endlessly stupendous, *unfathomable* reality, as diffused and grappled by the fleeting figures of mind. (There "is" not much else.) Within the Un-Order, humanity subsists in a virtual void, like a speck of dust lost in intergalactic space — amazingly, *profoundly* alone. The aware, the creative, *the intrepid homo sapiens!*

No one could have asked for this. In our time, each revelation of Truth has become a new question, an unenduring probability, a smoldering afterthought. Human reason and moral temperament will never again rest so securely nor grow so fully within the well-tended incubator of the "metaphysical explanation." (As if metaphysics could presuppose its own explanation!) It is *our* fortune to seek life in this forsaken, cold vacuum — we firstborn of the Third Millennium.

WHAT, ME WORRY?

Do I suffer from a defect of character because I aspire to be influential rather than authoritative? I would rather put minds and images in motion than lay them to rest.

Down in Doggsville, a more impulsive and repulsive face of knowledge emerges, where towers of solid, shifting substance teeter upon flimsy, florescent forms of glued-together adjectives (nouns in name only), *a foundation of mud* for titanic sandcastles in a bright, blue sky. Immovable universals devolve into the improvident angels of a rotting, regnant syntax. Ancient logic, brutish and indispensable, permeates the aesthetic. Our sense, our sovereign grasp, becomes the fool's reality.

ERROR TERM

In all probability, the Invisible Hand of the True Truth has it *totally* summed up for us, forever! *The whole enchilada!* From a first awareness to our final nothingness, it clutches closely to the most unsullied, subliminal assumptions ever devised. It waives away inquiry, it ordains the universal, and it rationalizes the Real. It keeps stitched tightly together, in a wild and woolly cosmos, the fundamental firmament for all possibly possible, intelligible intelligence. Odds are, it pounds coarse, ugly facts into harmless stardust. And with those magical digits, it molds perfect circles out of crumbling pyramids.

On the other hand, *any* curve-fitting regression of the imagination (especially this collectively conceived, omniscient, and omnipresent retainer of revelation) can be undone. The Invisible Hand conjures the incomparably inexplicable essence of substance, and it ossifies otherwise fantastic fictions. The unwavering, right hand of One-ness "corresponds" (huh?) "True Knowledge" (what?) to "Reality" (good grief!), while portraying to us huddled humans the transparency of existence and the timeless certitude of our fixed ideas — in an ontic instant, the cosmos gets flattened into an eternally present, physio-centric spacetime, imploding like a mind-mashing singularity with null for a denominator. But there is *nothing* rational nor relatable to say about a convergent universe-*in-itself* that subsumes the fullness of Being unto itself. It impresses no more, and it interests us less. We have come to envision that *all* language is local, any problem is parochial, and every last law is displaceable.

In other words, the Truly True Truth doesn't really *do* much, except for its being truly true. This requires no agency, invisible or otherwise, to affect Effects. Nothing gets *caused* by true Truth, beyond the continuing confirmation of humanity's *genuinely* necessary (life-sustaining) and unflinching belief that Existence exists, and that Reality gets realized in this "present tense" (as so, I think, do I). However, these days, we can't shake the feeling that something must be brewing within the poorly understood vertices conjoining past and future, nouns and verbs, Truth and Reality, subjective, objective, induction, deduction, Cause and Effect, etc. That brew might eventually be anointed (if past is prologue, and following further, endemic polemics) "to be" the more deeply dormitive power of an *even more truly*, True Truth! *Ad infinitum.*

What a mess! Let's step back . . . Human intelligence is *aesthetic* thinking. It is a neurologically constituted, naturally complemented, and linguistically perfected systemization of organic judgment — a never-ending delineation and verification of infinitely interrelatable, coalescing objects of interest, virtually animated, reduced and revealed by an *un*-Invisible Hand, the sinister visage and phantom agent of an *un*-envisionable mind (a colossally communal, ultra-linguistic, and thoroughly *anthropic* mind). Human need, and nothing else, affects human action. Life begets belief, and a restless, expansive intellect is the posterity of language. It is *the aesthetic of a species*, rather than a mathematician's intuition of transcendence, that engenders Truth.

And then, intelligence exudes irony and masks absurdity, as the Invisible Hand gathers from the good Earth, into divine, princely realms of pure reason and solid materiality, the random noise of raw reality. So jumping ahead, let's state the obvious: Logic (as we know it) is a *function* of consciousness — it is a *consequence* of language, a product of the psyche, and an instrument for the mind — and the cosmos is not.

Or consider this: (1) Without subjectivity, there can be doubt (Descartes); (2) Subjectivity is not objective (Kant); and (3) Each understanding, no matter how intuitive, analytic, fictitious, or false, is inextricably tethered to a *human* mind relating *human* hypotheses. (Dogg, Homer, ed., *The Sezyoo Compendium of Fancy Truisms.*)

As it were, scientific predictability is simply enchanting. (It is ever so statuesque!) And it pays the bills. Nevertheless, a reflection of the "uncertainty principle" underlies the very thinking about it, it inures to every bit of thought, and do *not* underestimate the power of uncertainty.

For example, wouldn't it also be ironic, "in the final analysis," if theoretical physics, instead of reducing itself further into the natural sciences, should explode itself out into theoretical psychology? And if the feats of physics are inexhaustibly incompletable, does the fault lie in our stars? — We shall rest assured, beneath billows of dark matter, that techno-gurus and super-square geometricians will forever after always get the first and last word in science. Or do you suppose there may be utterly *un*-explorable, immediate phenomena out there, shaping a consummately *un*-conceivable dynamic of inferences, which might circumscribe and settle, irrevocably and in perpetuity, the quintessential complex of limits to human understanding?

Naturally, there shall coexist, within a finely defined and finally confined uni-verse, an absolute, *epistemological* perfection of human understanding and the ultimate, *ontological* theory-of-everything. (Pardon my French.) So where would such perfection and such a theory be found? (*Not* in musty passages. Not with *our* nascent language.) The Holy Grail lies buried under megatons of ash, in a brutal, terrifying wilderness, and it's still a hundred thousand light years away — the ends of the universe are all but unexplored, so many generations are not yet born, and *so much* of the human experience remains invisible.

. . . *Slapped* in the face by the beloved Invisible Hand. What myth-maker or knowledge-mixer has not had to suppress this thought?

NUMEROLOGY

Zero and one are the magic numbers of reason. Division by zero and singularities are the magic numbers of the unimaginable. But these are only human fixations. God does not do math.

THE LADY
FROM EGYPT

The greatest genius of all time was a beautiful, fearless woman, who lived in Egypt about 5,500 years ago. She was irrepressibly curious, wholly self-possessed, and *acutely* impressionable. Also, she listened to the priests every chance she could get, and she observed their rituals, and everything else around her, with inspired mindfulness and *meticulous* creativity. On top of all this, she was a highly successful woman of the world. She directed scores of busy slaves, and she bartered daily on behalf of one of the largest households in all of Egypt. And so, in due time, she was exceedingly well-educated, and she had become an exceptionally seasoned and extremely skillful thinker.

During her contemplative moods, it frequently occurred to her that the world did not *have* to be a

hodgepodge of separate objects that were all inhab-
ited by a cacophony of animating demons and spirits,
as she had always been told, and as she always truly
believed. Perhaps instead, the world was "one," a uni-
verse, a single system, a "nature" that was, in a "higher
essence of truth," the reflection or product of a single,
omnipotent spirit.

The lady from Egypt (we should be clear about
this) did *not* become the greatest genius of all time
because she was the first to speculate on the possibility of God. She had simply succeeded the women and
men of genius, who painted on cave walls hundreds
of centuries before that, and many more besides, who
over the ages had more or less come up with the same,
inarticulable idea.

Yet her extraordinary genius shone, in every
aspect, as she *construed* and then *communicated* her
earth-shattering, outlandish and confusing idea to
priest and people alike, without being blatantly absurd
or making it sound too much like blasphemy. She had
seen that she was living among the first inhabitants of
a vast, new order, which was spreading rapidly along
the Nile. To those first generations, she presented the
idea so vividly and coherently that, this time around,
the idea would not die — at least not among the

philosophers and kings. The idea was tossed around for a couple of thousand years, and then, like a wind-blown wildfire, its tendrils spun into a celestial lace of divine revelation and illustrious poetry. Eventually, just about everyone believed the idea, and everything else fell into line.

THE LAST ACT

"God forgive me! God save me! Why *this*, God? Why *now*? Oh, my God! Why *meeeeee*!? Sweet, dear God, please . . . *please God forgive me all my sins!*"

> So screamed and sobbed
> the mission'ry,
> Who was sitting in 26-D,
> While the flaming jet-plane
> plummeted down,
> Into the icy sea.

Life is strange. The hysterical young man never had the chance to conceive that his pitiful begging was *useless* in the eyes of the Almighty, except to show finally the wanton shallowness of his God-fearing soul, and the bottomless conceits of a mind so willingly mired into blind faith.

YELLOW BRICK ROAD

If God wanted us to believe so firmly in the existence of a supreme being, in some guy, who made man in his own image, and who will come to judge the living and the dead, then He wouldn't have given us the brains, the heart, the nerve . . . we'rrrrrrre off!

THE RABBI'S RIDE

As the Rabbi approached Jerusalem, to his complete astonishment he was met by an adoring crowd. He was placed upon a donkey and led triumphantly into the city. The Rabbi was struck dumb by his consternation and disbelief. "How can this be?" he thought to himself, "I am being misunderstood!" The Rabbi realized he was doomed. And on the eve of his annihilation, he understood that he had failed them all.

POSTHUMOUS LIFE

God is dead.
And so is Nietzsche.
Hold it. Wait a minute!
I just remembered . . .
God *can't* be dead.
God is *inanimate*!
(But Nietzsche wasn't.)
God is love. God is dead.
Elvis lives.

THE LOVE
CONNECTION

All you *need*, is *love*!

Say, *what*? Isn't love the unconditional, bare minimum? And could you imagine that all you really *got*, is *life*!

Yeah, yeah, yeah . . .

The unloved die young. It is primordial that you should strive to love *thine own self*. If not, your neighbor and your lover could take you, and rightly so, for a sucking pig.

Not too much better are the confirmed neo-innocents who already love the whole world. Their experience of love has been crammed into a glorious, obvious, and everlasting notion, which they have bolted firmly inside their morally uplifted heads. For egotists and cheap thinkers, the love of one's self will wither into imperturbable dreams of sublimity, while any connection to the enraptured, heartrending passion for life has been lost to eternity. *Love is not* cozy satisfaction, no matter how serene and happy forever after.

And what would *you* know of love, or life, or yourself, if you have not permitted every ecstasy and anguish of love to permeate and tear into the far, unseen recesses of your soul. Has your most engaged, most *authentic* self been suffused with the nectar of existence — by the very feeling, that precious knowledge of *aliveness*? Or perhaps your whole being (this sentience in articulation) has erupted with a consuming, raging desire to share the meaning, peace, and pain of life with all who would be there with you — with all whom you would deeply wish to be there with you.

DEAD BOHEMIANS

I need the raw, undaunted pulse I get from city beats and downtown artists. But then I get disturbed by life on the edge, as if "the edge" were the last and only place.

You there, creative people! Why the confusion? Surely, you will live uselessly and die badly, if all your dreams must shine and rhyme.

And who said, "*Truth and Beauty shall Be forever!*"? Stop eating that horseshit. Death is an artless void. Until then, embrace the ephemeral while you lie down with cretins, again and again. Seek out tragedy and love, comedy and absurdity, one more time, and time again. *Keep moving*, or all decays into dust. Tread the foaming sea, or drown.

I'll say it, but you already know it. There is no peace, only peaceful moments, in a life of countless labors and fine creation.

BEAUTY AND
THE BEAST

There comes a time when an artist's sense of perfection degrades into meekness. They must dare to fail, or before the cock crows, every gift and talent will dry up and blow away.

It's not pretty. The artist must grind it through and sweat it out, *without* mercy, showing *no* pity, and maintaining (hopefully) some semblance of dignity, while they bang their aching head against walls and doors. Whatever the work, whatever they are seeking, the unquestioned artist requires method, discipline, and years of practice. They harbor an irrational, insatiable need to affix the rarest forms (the most pure and stunning visions) upon the cosmos, *and they must*, along the way, continue to produce. Believe it.

But do not believe these ancient Greeks. There are no gods of music. There is no sublime, divine creation. (Oh, lyrical lunacy!) All life began in the warm mud. *Mind* has evolved *out of matter*. A profound inspiration rises fitfully from the Earth.

THE EXAMINED LIFE

So I said to the mirror . . . If your message is ahead of its time and hard to understand, then maybe you're not so smart. Maybe your art is just too weak. Or maybe your method is lop-sided: Tell us, why did you stop digging? Don't you like to dig? And how can you be so composed, so sedate? Your language is convoluted and artificial. Your work is an imitation. Your idea is vague, a shadow on the wall. It lacks substance. It reflects very poorly some kindling flickers of bright, living light inside your head, which have, apparently, long since melted back into the hiding place.

Please excuse me. I do not mean to say that you are dishonest, deceiving, or mendacious. I mean to say that you *lie*. You lie to yourself and to everyone else who's supposed to believe that you offer anything more than a few chips and fragments behind that velvety curtain.

CREATIVE OBSESSION

I squandered the strength of my soul — a dozen times so far, maybe more — and I will do it *again*! If only I had the strength.

But I *will* have the strength again. I know it, you see, now I understand it — now that the most ingenuous and bewildering struggles are fading into mist and vapor. I will again be uprooted by this mind-pounding inspiration (a pulsing underground of crystallizing confusion), and I *will* be starkly, grimly challenged by another compelling vision, perhaps seeing the merest possibility of some *dazzlingly* original (gut-wrenching) work of art. Then once more, the foundations crumble beneath me, and I endure a twisting disorientation and free fall. Soon enough, I will slam down in an indulgence of dread and disgust, while before me lies only imperfect, ugly, disinterred bovinity — this time, I may have given it four or five days of frantic shoveling and nonstop panning, and for a few measly sketches (*nothing is working*), or else to forget it, forever. Still, I *must* experience these fervors again, all the exhilarating, immaculate revelations, and the privileged repose of a forebearing herald, a conduit and discerning *maestro* of human culture, a well-tuned, red-hot medium of meticulous, consequential, and *breathlessly* aesthetic tapestries. The visions form and I gasp. I am madly, desperately enthralled. I feel the pride and afterglow of a seemingly *flawless* realization, blessed once more with a thousand glistening discoveries and a richly unfolding masterpiece, the fruit of *my* inspiration and practice. Yes, this *sweet*, creative life! Yes, it is *true*! This process, knowledge, the world — it is art! *Civilization is art!* And humankind *is* the creator! The very creator and perpetrator of a sacred, higher existence!

But then I will feel the excruciating emptiness again, I will be *barren* again . . .

"Oh, this is absolute *nonsense*! He's just an uncouth poet, after all. That *awful* Mr. Dogg!" (I can suddenly hear the lady at the Garden Club saying). "And he is *so* vague and contradictory!" (What is this? — Where *am* I?)

"Madam, am I being vague?" (said the oncologist). "Am I being contradictory?" (said the hammer to the nail). Very well then, I will now *clearly* disclose my meaning to the whole world, close-up and butt naked, and here it is, the *real message*:

Pursue the arts, relentlessly! *Desire* these burdens, *savor* the intensity (a consummate magnificence, a *more profound* reality). *Cultivate perfection!* I *dare* you . . . No, wait! Pay no attention. What slop! (I'm tired, losing my focus.) For this work, I can dare *myself*, my own, sweet scrivening self, and that is enough, and . . . Yes! That's *it*! That *is* enough! — Oh, this fantastic obsession. My *beautiful* obsession. I must have more!

DEEP QUESTIONS

A person with a keen interest in art might eventually become interested in the question, "What *is* art?" — What is its real work, its driving purpose, its true nature? These questions concern the philosophy of art. Over the years, this person might also become interested in the philosophy of history, the philosophy of science, the philosophy of mind and language, etc., until driven to ask, "What *is* philosophy?"

This last question leads to an amusing interest in the philosophy of philosophy, which might also be refined, apparently, into a serious, lifelong study of "the *is*-ness of *Be*-ing." We can plaster-over our amusements with solemn language and grammatical gymnastics, but at some point we must also consider the impossibility that anything can genuinely explain itself — *any* explanation, if it is rational, could be nothing less than a comparison, it is the act of translating things and images into words and formulations, and to suppose uncritically that this question, "What *is* philosophy?" must aim at some essential Truth, is to risk a headlong plunge into an immeasurable, black whirlpool of absurdity. We must consider that there may not be much of an answer, which amounts to supposing that "What *is* philosophy?" may not be much of a question.

MACHETE

Swarms of magical *touristas* flit and flutter daintily from star to star, and with such *wonderful* feelings of safety, exclaiming "ooh!" and "aah!" at every burst of color and sensation.

Far below, deep within the interior of a remote jungle island, a small band of explorers pauses for a midday rest. They are already nine days in from the landing, and they have relentless, heartbreaking weeks of trekking yet to come. They rest without speaking, their eyes and ears sharp to every danger. They savor long drinks of warm, sweet tea. They slowly, coolly file their machetes to a razor's edge. And in a moment, they will move on, in another afternoon's orgy of sweat, fearing nothing, cutting deeper into the treacherous, so very beautiful interior.

That evening, the throngs will converge at the restaurant to discuss their dreams, while a continent away the exhausted explorers take their rations beneath the weathered tarp — yielding once more to the impending hours of unbroken darkness, preparing for their dreamless sleep and the next day's foray still deeper into the jungle's maddening, mysterious heart.

Will you, like a fluttering acolyte, philosophize with a needle and thread? Shall we sew it all together, until dinner, with a *left*, right, east and west, up and down, and over *again*? Do you beseech the Great Synthesis, the be-all and end-all, Unquestionable Answer?

Or will you, like the explorer, philosophize with a hammer, and with a machete. Will you cut your own path, traveling light, taking with you only — what it takes. It's time to decide.

Only one chance is the last chance, my friend. And this may be it. Make up your mind! Ignorance is hell. (*Idiocy* is bliss.)

FOUNTAIN OF VIRTUE

The incidental preservation of innocence: a curious side effect of getting strung-out on philosophy. To be a sophisticate, a savant, a worldly practitioner, a hardened traveler — and yet, to be an innocent, a square-pegged, wide-eyed truth-teller. This is *profoundly* virtuous.

. . . Isn't it? Or is it merely profoundly *difficult*? (Or maybe, a little *too* ridiculous?)

GRAFFITI

Nietzsche is peachy.

But Hegel's a bagel.

Voltaire! So spare!

   a square with flair.

Descartes! And Sartre!

   did part their hearts.

(*It's Kant* we want,

   not flaunts and taunts.)

Waldo waddles, Peirce is fierce,

James has flames he snarls

    in the Charles.

Locke doth talk, Russell's a tussle,

There's room to exhume Mr. Hume,

    I presume.

Schopenhauer — sour power!

Kierkegaard's — ironic petards!

Lustin' and trustin' — there goes St. Augustine!

And Heidegger — is full of shit.

PILGRIMS AND POSTULATES

Cast a cold eye on lily-livered cognoscenti and do-nothing scribblers. They wallow in murky, abstruse essences, while other, more gracious visitors, hone the experience and venerate the Earth.

Hold your horses, horseman, and don't pass by just yet. Tell me, why must we hunker under such vapid visions of existence and the parochial presumption of a final, first philosophy? Why do we grovel before eternally incorrigible, illusory propositions (these indulgent suppositions of certainty)? The postulation of a *dimensionless* Reality is no burden for those who abide a soaring faith in the *temporality of the aesthetic* and in the absolute contingency of all worlds. Go tell these pilgrims, "God is dead!" and they'll say, "Big Deal!" "Who cares?" and "So what?" Then if you don't leave they might ask you, "So, what's *next*, genius?"

THE SUFFICIENCY
OF REASON

That a "sufficient reason" exists for everything we could ever put our minds to, is just an ugly truism, gussied-up like a beautiful principle.

That our perception of effects is the *sum and substance* of our concept of a cause, is a downright beautiful truism, which comes in the guise of an ugly principle.

TRUTH AND CONSEQUENCES

Human logic is rooted in four dimensions. The cosmos is not so limited — nonetheless, the "cash value" of pure truth is that we humans have come to share an immovable knowledge that certain things should always go together — like entropy and time, force and motion, experience/memory, love to tears, and life unto death. It remains a matter of pure *faith*, however, that reality reigns presently, and that the future conforms eternally to the cycles of our past.

Look back (look *everywhere*) you honest priests of Plato. Somewhere beside our pure and perfect faith, far within these endless caverns, you will rediscover the ancient rhyme and center of the universe.

THE ASSIMILATION

Each mind: An *assimilation*, a vast accretion of sensing, perceiving, doubting, conceiving; a viscid cauldron of mixing memory, volatile and fuming, radically unique, virtually *infinite* intricacies; an infinitude.

The manifest, terminable interest.

Humanity: Minds conjoined, *each to each* (beings in their billions, across a thousand ages), bound by relentless temporalities and embraced in a timeless transaction, affirmed, *confirmed* by the living languages — word upon word, mind into mind, *the assimilation of assimilations* compounding perpetually, reflecting incessantly within itself, an *inconceivable*, godlike complexity, in and of each self — *the infinitude, factorial!*

Our paltry equal to the cosmos.

This *monstrous* complexity. The unholy Leviathan! Fed by language, tamed by language, perfected by language. And so, a beginning: The perceptible, the *communicable*, the fundaments of knowledge — cascading, brain-based molecules of intensifying intellect across the revolving mirrors of a *shared aesthetic*, the irrepressible arrays of our common transcendence — *worlds* materializing, true images admixed, casting spectral, unquietable portraits of an utterly anthropic uni-verse. Forging and forming, bit by bit, vision by vision, inexorably, to the last.

The present: an inchoate hypothesis. The future, mere faith. (Only what is past is intelligible.)

TESTIMONY

The average man of refinement will settle into his high-towered bastion, a place where he can look down, safe from all the riff-raff, at leisure to write and think, surrounded by his music, books, wine, and equally refined acquaintances. From that exalted retreat, he may disregard the sprawling worlds below, as he shelters unperturbed by rough realities and coarse objections. Secure in his knowledge and comfortably ensconced, so begins his slow, dreadful degeneration.

The exceptional man of refinement keeps hard, fertile ground beneath his feet. In bohemian bars, sweaty offices and on back roads, in the company of innocents, renegades, lunatics and fanatics, he wages a singular, masterful reply to this predicament of existence. He seeks the rarest nuances of the human drama, to attain a more genuine understanding, *to bear witness* more astutely to so much brief and impassioned life.

From the unfinished work of dying artists, he sharpens his sense of tragedy. With primitives he unearths the primordial, while among the faith-addicted, he beholds everlasting wells of irony. In the halls of practitioners, he understands to reserve each judgment. From criminals and thieves also, he observes the art of cool.

The exceptional man of refinement measures each deed against the rolling tides and bare facts of terrestrial life. He is borne by a deliberate virtue and a scholarly, hard-won discipline. He walks the Earth in quiet elegance, for a moment's grace, as a true philosopher.

FADING MEMORIES

If you come to some breathtaking or soul-bending location, and you want to take the view home with you, then buy an extra postcard. But the view un-trumps the postcard, and don't you forget it, when you're standing face to face with something worth seeing.

There's no such thing as traveling back. Always take a good look. Every look is a last look.

SILENT NIGHT

Dear Friends,

I met a French poet in Banjarmasin. She'd been on the road about seven or eight years. She told inspired, amazing stories, and this was her prayer . . .

"I swear to every god there is, and to every man and every woman who ever has, or ever will draw breath upon the Earth — I swear that I will temper this shattering creativity with perfection and virtue, that I will make my art a work of life and my life a work of art, that I will seek knowledge from every quarter, nurture the young, and *never* resist a generous impulse. May humanity flourish — and may I die without regret, amen."

Sincerely yours,

Farewell,
Homer Dogg

CREATIVE OBSESSION

AFTERWORD

Creative Obsession comprises copious, simmering segments of variegated aphorisms, apothegms, and apologues. Each segment is discrete work, however, the profusion of pieces imparts images and points of light upon a pervasive matrix of allusions, which imbues dynamic apperceptions of a transcendent, meticulous whole. A severe economy of words provides this matrix with a semblance of immediacy, eliciting a conceptual undercurrent that reflects a primal and subliminal apprehension of the *raging interexistence* (the quintessential simultaneity) of aesthetic, epistemic, and ethic thinking. Whew.

— APHORISTIC —

The aphorism is artwork of fastidiously refined, didactic prose that is punctuated by metaphoric language, the elucidation of philosophic experience, and brevity. The rare possibilities of authentic, aphoristic originality constrain the writer to ponder protolinguistically, while resorting methodically and *seamlessly* to every tool and competency of the rhetorical art. The reader of aphorisms, if he or she is systematically inclined, may wish to identify the various syntheses of interlaced figures formed by meiosis and metonymy, allegory and alliteration, or chiasmus, synecdoche, verisimilitude, and so on.

An emergent aphorism might materialize in the midst of mixing, undulating apparitions and translucent fusions getting wrung through opposing perlocutions of figure and modality (what?) — *volatile* amalgams that, when first conceived, evoke palpable, yet strewn and shapeless intuitions of profound understanding. Then a mastery of composition and every power of improvisation at the artist's disposal must be exactly invoked, to discern whether this ethereal vision might be brought into communion with the unyielding enigma of human intelligence, or is just another figment (trite and thoroughly subjective), one glimpse and it's gone forever, one more misty memory.

The pivotal labor of the aphorism writer is to uncover new figures of speech, or new juxtapositions of meaning, mode, mood, and meter, which convey seemingly immeasurable realizations concisely and with pronounced effect. Communication of this nature entails a particularly judicious and efficient use of language. Ideally, an incisive narrative engenders a series of distinct images, erupting magnificently into being at the frontiers of the mind, near the harrowing abyss of utter incoherency — so to speak. In the beginning, these images could be sparked by a simple simile or a stunningly apt metaphor. A thousand pictures launched with a single word — that is the ultimate goal of the aphorism writer.

The foreboding edge of experience, if fairly captured and reduced to language, can produce fantastically unintended assimilations wrapped in compounding ironies, elegant consistencies, and prolific resonance. The aphorism may disarm the reader with subtle, or perhaps jarring changes of mood and subject, or the author reveals enduring predicaments, which allow familiar and receptive frames of mind, so that reader and author engage effortlessly, unaffectedly, and with uncommon depth and intimacy. But then the reader may be led blithely along a winding path, only to be left alone, at the critical juncture, to fend in solitude.[1]

As far as *figure reflects vision and form follows figure* (ethic), aphoristic work might complement more intricate *frames of validity* (aesthetic). To dig for aphorisms is *to try one's knowledge* of the most elusive percepts and inexplicable recurrences (epistemic).

And then brick by brick, layer upon layer, aphoristic work attains a smoking mass that is encompassed, insofar as it is *delimited* by scrupulous depictions of pure creativity and unfettered spontaneity (a nebulous mirror in a dimensionless cosmos), by means of expansive, organic processes (the synapses, brainwaves and consonant symmetries of outlying ideas and correlative concepts), through which the work becomes organic in itself, as a systemic embodiment, the "whole," subsumes its parts. The writer's shadow dissolves into the burgeoning, hermeneutic "circles" of such finely transposing rhetoric, and where we surmise no clear sight nor sense of a restrictive, autonomous authorship, the reader may find, from the depths of a perfected

---

1. Oden, T.C., ed., *Parables of Kierkegaard* (Princeton Univ. Press, 1978), pp. viii-xii.

aphorism, that time and circumstance grow increasingly immaterial. That is, subject, reader, author and aphorism become virtually nondistinguishable.

. . .

Creative Obsession demonstrates that aphoristic forms can be as richly varied as people's noses, although in modern English, the "aphorism" is one more tightly defined and impressive-sounding noun that would have worked better as an adjective. Blooms of nuanced impressions and promising premonitions (for example, the *"aporistic"* potential of *aphoristic* prose) fade quickly into overused and quasi-meaningless words (words that attract lots of synonyms), simply because we talk too much. These days, "aphorism" usually signifies pithy, philosophical proverbs (or quips, adages, epigrams, witticisms, etc.) such as, "A winner never quits, and a quitter never wins."

A poignant proverb may be aphoristic, and at some point, a proverb is more properly termed an *apothegm*. In my view, the apothegm is a kind of aphorism. It is an extremely brief aphorism. However, apothegms are often less evocative philosophically, if not saccharine and insipid, and even the niftiest ditties will seldom exhibit the final refinements of fully integrated prose. Many semi-apothegmicals get embedded in drama-starved creations, while overly ambitious apothegms frequently conceal bizarre tautologies and *non sequiturs*. In the annals and catacombs of cultivated language, profound and discrete apothegms are exceedingly rare.

The *apologue*, like the apothegm, is a kind of aphorism. It is an aphoristic *fable*, and a timeless, flashy fable is *The Tortoise and the Hare*. But it would be garish to reinfuse that famously familiar fantasy with pilfered piles of swag and bags of blinding bling, so that it might mimic an apologue. It is truly difficult, in an age of undying fictions, to illuminate elegant facets of the apologue. The sketches are invariably sappy, easily dated, or too long. The allegory is typically transparent, and seamless textures may belie subtle contrivances.

The standard aphorism, if there is such a thing, is an aphoristic *abstract* (all vignette and *no* twaddle). It is made from densely worded, highly cohesive prose that precisely stuffs the spaces displaced by the efficient, protolinguistic crystallization of our most wildly evasive ideas. It is neither an apothegm nor an apologue, even though many standard aphorisms will exude traces of the apothegm and the apologue.

That's it. That's all the useful labeling around here. And thousands of aphoristic forms remain undiscovered. *They will be revealed*, perhaps, by our unquenched passions and the inexorable tides of meticulous and *effective* methods of art.

I may lack deference to, but hopefully not respect for my native language, and so I conveniently (*not* definitively?) refer to these scattered compositions as "aphorisms," and I try to distinguish the forms of aphorisms, which are derived from the art of speech called rhetoric, from the countless forms of expression derived from that other art of speech called poetry.

— PHILOSOPHIC —

The command to "question authority" would seem indispensable to rigorous inquiry. But to *question* authority is pointless, unless there is a correlative *resort* to authority. Any scientist or lawyer will tell you that in complex, sensitive and high stakes situations, adversaries will come to blows, without some fundamental, rationalizing agreement on authorities, whether that authority is the law of gravity or the law of contracts.

And so I feel in step, when I cite Kant and Nietzsche (odd bedfellows) as the irreproachable authorities for humankind's decisive encounter (win or lose) with the labyrinths of language, with these *life-sustaining adaptations* of the collective mind, our *creation of meaning,* or as the good philosophers more precisely envision it, *"the arts of speech are rhetoric and poetry."*[2]

> "Rhetoric is the art of transacting a
> serious business of the understanding as
> if it were a free play of the imagination;
> poetry of conducting a free play of the
> imagination as if it were a serious busi-
> ness of the understanding."[3]

Without question, philosophy is a serious (consequential) business of the understanding. Good (and widely understood) philosophy has, more than once, drawn civilization toward the flower of enlightened democracy, and meanwhile, bad philosophy is the demon midwife of all crimes against humanity, from

---

2. Nietzsche, F. W., *Description of Ancient Rhetoric,* (Gilman, S.L., *et al.,* eds.), *Friedrich Nietzsche on Rhetoric and Language* (Oxford Univ. Press, 1989), p. 3 [emphasis added].
3. *Id.*

the assassination of Socrates to the Holocaust. On the other hand, the *act* of philosophizing — which, like cloud-gazing, is a distinguishing pastime for otherwise occupied humans, from the aristocratic Plato to his Thracian slave — remains a boundless and airy undertaking of the imagination. Therefore, given that philosophy is a transaction of the understanding, it follows that the language of philosophy (*par excellence*) is *the art of rhetoric.*

(Incidentally, did my syllogistically inspired ritual, just now, leave your stomach half-empty? Yes? So why does the formalization of philosophic insight tend to make us feel like somebody is feeding us loaves of Wonder Bread? When we are painfully honest and crystal clear, we come to the stultifying conclusion that in *any* argumentative or theoretical monologue, whether an airtight *tour de force* or a lousy load of leaky logic, we are ultimately "begging the question" presented by our unprovable postulates and *incompletable* (Gödelian) systems. This is, to say the least, a domain-shrinking realization and a problematic constraint. Likewise, in our zeal to be logically impregnable, eternally certain, omni-analytical, and *pan-theoretical* — to be, that is, dramatically and indisputably "universal" — if we allow our stated, unstated, and preconscious premises to become hopelessly meshed and crushed within the tentacles of a sumptuous, obscure construct, we may not appreciate the collapsing cognitive confines displaced by the dilapidating dialectics and stripped-down analytics, nor the implicit, moldering circularity entrenched so thoroughly throughout such suffocating, dressed-up Truth. And in the confusion, we invite gross error or the temptation — the original sin — to delve deeper into capricious, curve-fitting distinctions and superior obscurity.)

Thank you for allowing me to get that off my chest. To continue, I am of course referring to the art of rhetoric, in the sense of that distinguished, ancient practice of *public discourse* (and its scholarly progeny), held in orderly, peaceful, and public places by a sovereign people, as opposed to the base "rhetoric" of unschooled lawyers and mendacious politicians.

However, what is often *less* apparent, is that the rhetorical is not merely informed by the critical analysis of artistic modalities of speaking and writing. To paraphrase Nietzsche, rhetoric has also always existed as a *preconscious art* in our use of language.[4] In the protolinguistic recesses of the mind, especially among children and the young, rhetoric elicits *a continuous*

---

4. *See* Nietzsche, F. W., *Description of Ancient Rhetoric, op. cit.*, p. 21.

aesthetic awakening (a precious radiance), as each person discovers words and webs that work and impress, concerning ever more intricate objects of increasingly intense interest.

Rhetoric is a deliberate, collaborative, and incendiary art. It complements the emergent consciousness, and for immeasurable millennia, it has imbued its primal form of meaning upon the human soul. So in lucid moments, I might freely imagine a group of inventive and intelligent Paleolithic teenagers, sitting around one of their amazing, manufactured fires, and in closeknit communication, they all came to understand that the figurative exclamation, "YEE-aag!" would from then on signify a blazing "Hot-Mama!" and that "Umm-umm-BOH" would mean that somebody cool had gotten a little ying-yang. Later generations (*tireless*, creative youth) would similarly assimilate these exquisitely descriptive terms, while experiencing mind-altering, aesthetic pleasure through their language's communal usage, consistent grammar, and seemingly unbounded powers of expression.

But all beauty decays, and soon enough the repetitive uses, misuses, and habits of language will meld what was once rhetorically luminous into a loopy mash of moribund concepts.

Nietzsche was characteristically circumspect regarding his choice of words. So it is all the more astonishing when he asserts flatly that "language itself is the result of purely rhetorical arts," and that the human power of rhetoric is *the essence of language*."[5] For Nietzsche, and I might as well agree with him, we may write the dullest and the most precise abstracts, or fastidiously unbiased briefs, but there is no such thing as a "neutral" analysis or an unrhetorical, "natural" language.[6] The root of the word "fire" presumably began as a very ancient figure of speech. Even the numeral 2, which seems so completely inert, is completely rhetorical. It is, after all is said and done, an incalculable improvement over the numeral formerly known as II, for conveying the mathematical construct of two-ness.[7]

A solidly ingrained and *hypostatizing*, neo-natural language reflects (with proto-mathematical exactness) our most intractable habits of mind, those virtually invariant, everyday ideas we *inhabit*, without which we would be doomed to an autistic hell of ceaseless,

---

5. *Id.* [emphasis added].
6. Nietzsche, F. W., *Description of Ancient Rhetoric, op. cit.* p. 21.
7. *See* Peirce, C. S., *How to Make Our Ideas Clear*, Buchler, J., ed., *Philosophical Writings of Peirce* (Dover, 1955), pp. 35-36, and *Lowell Lectures on the History of Science*, Wiener, P., ed., *Charles S. Peirce: Selected Writings* (Dover, 1966), pp. 234-235.

faithless, mundane inquiry. That's why the large, bright appliance on the ceiling is just another "light" and not a puzzling, metaphysical difficulty, like it was when we were six days old. And our *inextricably fixed,* supposedly *a priori* habits of mind (for example, that some "*I*" thinks, or that "*I*" am) are functions of (are "caused" by) perfectible (communicable) and eternalistic (inalterable) linguistic webs, transposing like hard rocks out of reverberating patterns of experience.

Individual and communal experience is not the indeterminate set of every "real thing" (or other sufficiently singular percept) that has ever affected somebody's brain. For a knowing species, "experience" is better expressed as a verb, a modifier, or something in between. It is whatever we happen to attain, sustain, restrain and retain, whereas underlying the unavoidable constraints and deficiencies of perception, memory, language and logic, the core function of thinking is *inquiry* (in general, the mind's encounter with any sort of disequilibrium) and *judgment* (its correlative response).[8] Human intelligence acts upon mammoth aggregations of simple, complex, and profound judgments, which

---

8. *See* Dewey, J., *Logic: The Theory of Inquiry* (Harcourt, *et al.*, 1938), Ch. VI-VII, *accord*, Burke, F. T., *Dewey's New Logic* (Univ. of Chicago Press, 1998), pp. 136-146.

follows an adaptive, primordial obsession to advance finer pictures of our memories and more perfect habits of mind.[9] When such *teleoaesthetic* (regenerative and *divergent*) motives are in play, the exercise of the intellect may be called a "work of art." When we attempt, by mere words, to affect existing habits of mind, we are engaged in the art of rhetoric.

. . .

Language does not define Reality, nor does it describe the essence of Existence. We should not presume to be so eloquent, nor shrink from what is truly momentous: Language perfects facts. It is a lattice of our own making, through which intertwine immense compendia of ephemeral and ineffaceable points of agreement. From those first cries to the last word, language traces the aesthetic, delimits the object, and delineates worlds — from the subliminal to the hyperconscious, language renders memorable and communicable the

---

9. In this sense, "perfection" is the collective apprehension of a more fully resolved, intrinsic purpose (akin to the perfection of legal interests), rather than a static and unexceptional notion of immutable flawlessness (like my fuzzy vision of a perfect circle).

abductive inferences (things, ideas, "raw feels," etc.) that someone experiences *grammatically* (presently, subjectively, meaningfully). Accordingly, I could be sitting next to yet *another* fire, toasting my marshmallows, telling the guy next to me that the fire was *really* and *truly* hot, but if that fine fellow were trying to make high carbon steel, she might insist that the fire was as cold as hell. Therefore, no matter how intemperate the discussion, it is not the "essence" of fire to be hot *and* cold, to make us feel cozy, nor to forge steel, any more than it is the essence of fire to be called "fire." (Sadly, impeccable arguments and weighty conjunctions settle cases and controversies *only*. Our minds and manners are another matter.)

Writers delude themselves that they merely describe the things in their heads. However, readers do not doubt that each modern mind is the consequence of a written language. And thinkers think that memory is an *autolinguistic discussion* (the experience of consciousness) that one keeps having with oneself. Whether by words, recordings, memories, or telepathy, human language is a human tool, molding human minds for human needs. Wandering ponderers and virtuoso scholars do *not* receive, perceive, and conceive exalted, esoteric essences from sunny, far-off Transcendencia, so that they might adequately utter sentences corresponding truthfully to some *necessarily* real and thereby *ingeniously* christened Things-in-Themselves! (This sordid sort of lilting language is affectatious, pure poetry — *nobody* actually thinks this way.) But in fact, we *do* receive countless trillions of pixelated, chemo-neurological impulses, which the abductive mind fashions *aporistically* into sensations, memories, concepts, and in due course, our presumptively preconditioned, nominally mediated, fictive, certain, and *indelible* apperceptions of Reality.[10] We do not communicate sensations, apperceptions, fact-free analyses, Truth, nor any other matter of the mind, so much as we offer smattered *facsimiles* of our reasonably stable impressions, using "signs" (compelling images, familiar smells, and well-placed words make good signs) that bit by byte, further conjure ideas and fix memories, in the intermixing milieux of humanity's ultra-connective unconscious.

These bit-based, neural networks (the pointillistic mind-movies of thinking) *crystallize* selectively and progressively, first into bare awareness, then into

---

10. *See* James, W., *Some Problems of Philosophy* (Bison Books, 1996), pp. 47-112 (percept and concept).

mosaics of intensifying intelligence, and culminate with humankind's timelessly finite and conventionally unassailable systems of belief. The brain's crystallizations — perhaps swirling out of ecstatic rapture, inspired quietude, or dull habit — provide a more palatable, poetic veneer for a pervasive *"veritivity,"* a molecular meta-metaphor that stirs-up notions about *how* we get to True knowledge (instead *of what* it must consist). According to the hair-splitters, veritivity "warrants" (justifies) "assertible" (true enough, one way or another) "judgments" (conclusions), which range exhaustively, from baby's primitive, protolinguistic perception of "light," to the most math-meddling methods of philosophical analysis, to the fully formal, fictional, and *final* findings of fact adjudicated in hotly contested legal proceedings. Practitioners meticulously observe that veritivity shapes the interminable, reshuffling judgments of pure logic, punctilious dialectic, farce, poetry, dreams, etc.

So much delicate hair-splitting leads to bald spots and blunt results. Veritivity treats True knowledge as *the product of a process* (Truth being *functional*), rather than some static, question-begging relation ("correspondence") to Reality. And with no more instant Reality, it's getting uncomfortably obvious that the Truly True

Truth is thoroughly absurd, and not just ubiquitous. Also, veritivity manifests an inherent *communicability* of Truth (like mathematical properties attaching to numbers, *after* we've learned to count). Wrapped in time and riding the odds, *Veritivity unto Truth* is delimited by — coextensively, it is communicated *as* — the arts of creation (method) and the sciences of nature (knowledge), stewed in the hot pots and fat vats of language. In a strikingly restrictive mélange of meaning, the flowing crystallizations and dissipations of veritivity, comprising "hub-like" vertices (the nuclei of Truth), materialize in an earthly ether, across vast assimilations of sciencey facts and artsy arguments, spanning *open and unbounded sets* of abductively reconstructed, linguistic amplifications — these probabalistic and *measurable* (comparable, rational) molecules of mind *transposed* through sequences of neurologically propagating and aporistically apprehended, reverberating "spokes" and revealing to the intellect a *fully naturalized logic* — this Truth, and all that goes with it, gets "existed," so to speak, inside out from the outside in. Consequently, the communicability of The Truth, like the experience-ability of The Real, efficiently impresses upon each mind the fundamentally "un-subjective" (meta-metaphorical) situs, source, and substance of knowledge. In *this* light (the latent glow of humanity's disrupted, "heliocentric turn"), Existence-in-Itself is a *postulate*, any humanly imaginable Uni-verse is *incompletable*, "Being" morphs into a transitive verb, and Truth becomes quintessentially communal (*not* simply heavenly).

Meanwhile, back in my brain, and for as long as I can remember, my sentience keeps sliding into one big, solid and exceedingly clear *inference*, appearing unremittingly real and continuously, intuitively *substantive*, as the hypothetic genesis, probabalistic antecedents, and deducible consequences of "warrantably assertible" ideas permeate and subsume complementary subprocesses of pragmatic dialectic, conceptual hypostatization, and contextual disambiguation. (Whew, again!) Veritivity aligns our evolving neurophysiology to the precarious, malleable edge and probabilistic dictates (the sub-cosmic, existential predicament) of every conceivable world. This naturalized, "new logic" is not merely prescriptive, it is *methodologically suggestive* — in the twisting, unorientable domains of an edgeless universe, Truth becomes *conjunctive and adaptive* (creative) rather than *discursive and final* (authoritative).

If the neuroscientists and poets ever produce offspring, we'll get unimagined insights into the "grammar" (broadly conceived) of "veritivity" (even more broadly conceived). I've come to believe (which means I'm still speculating, but less indistinctly, more habitually, and on steroids) that a *grammar of veritivity*, starting (and ending) with a rock-solid description of the neurocognitive basis of creativity, may be envisioned from the far reaches as having evolved over one hundred fifty thousand generations (across the eternalistic ecstasies of existence and the unforgotten anguish of dying cultures and extinct human species) into a hardwired, autonomously motive, self-reprogrammable BIOS of the brain. In the ages of intercommunication yet to come, a grammar of veritivity may supplant language and logic as our primary interface with knowledge. Until then, our woefully imperfect, however scrupulously honest understanding of rhetorical methodologies and grammatic constraints, is what the early Ancients called *wisdom* (and respectfully, so do I).

Veritivity mediates the confluence of *fact* (aggregations of effects) and *logic* (memories of consequences), and returns diverging emanations of crystal clear cognizance (more facts) and distinct, conclusive consequences (more logic). Like mapped-out sequences of DNA, a grammar of veritivity *predicts* the tornadic transpositions of language and *controls* the ensuing, homeomorphic progressions of the mind. It channels an aporistic acuity that sculpts our metaphoric memories of scientific certainties, for example, of an immovable, flat Earth. It molds the undulating conglomerations and sums of vertices, out of the genome of each vertex, from which thinking conjoins and visions materialize. Grammatic inquiry probes the naturally extradimensional, reciprocating displacements of these uncountably infinite centerpoints of existence, inciting an incisive, consuming contemplation of the enveloping domains of *potential* creation — *all* of which is one more miniscule, soulful sentience in a *gargantuan* process of assimilation. (Or if you're in a hurry, just say "therefore," and then say, "I am.") Our more perfect description of how matters of intensifying interest "hang together," constitutes a more general and *actionable* (philosophical) understanding of True knowledge.

. . .

All that is known and knowable, like facts, things, fictions, and hallucinations, in other words, the *objects* of thinking (including me), from this red chair, to redness, to life's crimson dreams, are *a bundle of properties*, a bucket of objects relating to other objects, describable in words, grunts, gestures, mental activities, etc. winding through all kinds of contexts and activities, that is, into "sentences" (unsettleable sets of possible propositions), so at rock bottom, *all description is metaphorical.* Amassing memories meld seething similes into literal language, and from the primitive core to the bleeding edge, knowledge is "a flux of continually changing relations." It is "an infinitely large, and forever expansible, *web of relations* to other objects," which goes "all the way down and all the way out in every direction . . . [everything is] just one more nexus of relations."[11] This frameless web for the *objective* mode of knowledge is perfected by personal and interpersonal apperceptions of aesthetic cohesion among the crystalizing impressions, projecting bell curves of belief out of probabilistic peculiarities (shaping *habits of behavior* for a precarious planet). The impression is *inductive*, the object is *deductive*, and in between, the "crystallization" (the apotheosis of metaphor as logical hypothesis) is *abductive*. An ever-diverging knowledge is sustained by the endless issue of interweaving tendencies riddled with randomness. It is *not* grounded by preemptive, indubitable distinctions. Our knowledge congeals out of resonating *effects*, it is the culminating

---

11. Rorty, R. M., *Pragmatism as Anti-Authoritarianism* (Belknap, 2021), pp. 88-89, *see* pp. 84-103 (pan-relationalism) [emphasis added].

consequence of triadic, logical relations, and *every relation is an implicit predicate.* "[There] is nothing to be known about anything save what is stated in sentences describing it."[12] Language relates relating relations, like cascading reflections trapped in flowing fields of facing mirrors. Human knowledge is a thoroughly linguistic portraiture, drawn from the labyrinthine progressions and manifold meanings of rhetoric. It begins abductively, and it builds pointillistically, recycling and reverberating among the parts, wholes, and hermeneutic histories of every object. We create these worlds *aporistically,* with subliminal symbolism, ostensive description, and *effective* figures of speech.

In itself, Experience is not *knowledge* and Reason *makes* nothing true. Nor is Being the converging *essence* of it all. Meaningful, i.e. *useful* behaviors (such as walking, talking, thinking, etc.) *resolve organic needs* — and that's it. But, like a good whack on the head or a consciousness-altering epiphany, the never-ending adversities of life-in-nature (the earth-moving, mind-molding matrices of behavior) *cause* our perceptions of change and conceptions of choice (from the purely physiological to the radically creative, whether

---

12. *Ibid.,* p. 89

beautifully attractive or grotesquely repulsive), and engender our grammatically formed, hypostatized inferences of each and every world and object. Thought itself is *naturally selected* (actually, *organisms* do the selecting, "nature" doesn't care) and *species-specific*. The probabilistically discernible and intrinsically linguistic objects of knowledge are patterned by particles of description conjoined in aesthetically constrained waves of understanding, *e pluribus unum*. In the end, a "common preconsciousness" (the *residuum* of our reassimilating assimilations) further infuses and amplifies a fragile domain of humanistic holism, unspeakably suspended in cosmic dimensionless-ness. From the post-metaphysical perspective, "empiricism" is simply a simplifying rhetoric, and "realism" remains a rationalist myth. Every fact is refinable, any judgment is fictive, and for us to live and thrive in un-universal, *neo-philosophic* worlds, if we shall act, *then first we must believe* (each to their own), as much as we must breathe.[13]

And then, I exhale. Beyond my fleeting faith, there *is* no "question of Being." Existence-in-Fact is a concert of the living.

Billions of intercommunicating souls, enduring the tears and terrors of untold millennia, all desperately

---

13. *Ibid.*, pp. 24-46 (romantic polytheism).

seeking Truth (as much as they love life), will presumably leave tracks of surging ideas and dissipating
webs of meaning. And so a historical hypothesis is
the first impetus of the philosophic. The question
now is our redescription of an *adaptive* knowledge for
a distressed species on an increasingly inhospitable
planet. The matter is ripe, it is at-issue, and humankind must proceed, utterly unprepared for trial. The
artists have scarcely begun to reveal vague outlines for
a more predictive and not so conclusive Truth for the
impending epoch. Undaunted, their constant incur-
sions, far within the extradimensional purviews and
along the murky pathways blazed beneath a *virtually*
singular universe — their incessant spiraling through
the vertiginous centerpoints of reality and into the
reciprocating vertices of linguistically assimilating proto-
cognitions — promulgate arduous, mind-expanding
engagements with *the common preconsciousness of creative consequence* (what?) comprising immeasurable
nebulae of "heavy" (vision-intensive), poignant possibilities and potentially communicable figments, all
recycling and remixing inexorably, while unearthing
an *interminably* ever more complex cosmos (an encounter with Reality limited only by the conceivable). The
common preconsciousness of creative consequence is

the manifest medium for an impassioned, meticulously examined experience of a not-so-dismissably "instinctive," intergenerational knowledge of the knowable that we Moderns call *humanity*. Existence-in-Itself is weightless and merely eternal, however an overarching grammar of veritivity is effective and temporal. The churning crystallizations imbue the brain as they inform the mind immediately ("irreducibly"), consistently ("probabilistically"), and immersively ("aporistically"). Grammatic transcendence is a window into the soul of a living, growing *species of mind* — I'll be long dead before I distinctly behold this mastermind-in-reflection (if ever), but the exclusively human experience of humanity *also* has a heavy name, *"the aesthetic."* And every baby, philosopher, and litigant has felt it.

Indubitability is an annoying fetish. This much is given: *Thinking exists*, and *that's enough*, in particular, for postmodern (let me know when we get there) philosophic life. The formerly fundamental firmament of super-evident Truth is stale, thin air, wafting into a new millennium, dangling like an inactionable ornament, and patently useless to the logicians, rhetoricians, and poets of the finer arts.[14] Instead, a sub-theoretical,

---

14. *See* Rorty, R. M., *Consequences of Pragmatism* (Univ. of Minnesota Press, 1982), pp. xxxvii-xliv.

meta-metaphorical notion of *veritivity*, illuminating every *functional vertex* (the extradimensional "black box") for the perfectible, reverberating vectors — these triadic, emanating fusions of past and future (the present), inquiry to judgment (logic), induction/deduction (abduction), subjective vs. objective (who, me?), mind and behavior (language), Cause and Effect (existence), and I'll bet there's more — presents an immense and communicable, creative framework, a seemingly everlasting well of originality, and a wide-open path to a boundlessly astounding, nurturing, and flourishing human culture, in effect, *a refined understanding of the aesthetic.* Each human being's grammatic crystallizations interpolate swaths of coalescing phenomena and entangling intensions (where *am* I?), further propagating protolinguistically and inculcating in parallel a *communal* mind, reason, conscience and consciousness, *ex post facto* (which almost means *"a posteriori,"* except now there's more action and less backside), and forming a wholly human *Sitzplatz*, this *sacred* (and I mean just that) cathedra of Reality.

This is how we create Truth: rationally. Which also means selectively, communally, lovingly, and obsessively. Veritivity is *rational adaptation.* It is our survival. *We compare and we choose.* (In God we trust.)

In *our* time, during these few, mortal moments that homo sapiens shall walk the Earth, our place in a dimensionless, incognizable cosmos has been irrevocably, invisibly handed *to* humans *by* humanity, like a cold slap in the face. And at last, a quasi-magical contrivance (a *servile* Existence-in-Itself), this bloodless "Be-ing" through time, becomes known to us here-beings as a lame, bootstrapped tautology (in a single word!) — a *nonjusticiable*, yet utmost fictitious affair.

. . .

So if I observe, "the stone is hard," that does not establish the stone's hardness as something surpassing a physiologically abduced *judgment* on my part.[15] The recollection of hardness and other judgments of color, texture, size, unity, and so on, are constituents of the imagery elicited by the word "stone." (I mean, our language necessitates *predicates*, but reality takes care of itself.) When I say "stone," my listener subliminally imagines a "hard" object, or so I subliminally assume.

---

15. Nietzsche, F. W., *Description of Ancient Rhetoric, op. cit.*, p. 25; Pierce, C. S., *Chance, Love, and Logic* (Bison Books, 1998), pp. 42-47.

And as my meanings become progressively universal, my assumptions get more subliminal. It would thus be presumptuous to conclude that "the stone" (as referent) *intrinsically* caused that unforgettable and undeniably concrete sensation of hardness, and likewise, that YEE-aag! was the cause of hot! *and* cold! Still, unless I'm taking this to the edge, into the wild borderlands of rational description and fine writing, I don't much care — it was hot enough *already*, forever and everywhere, I sincerely believe.

Perhaps my sincere belief *does* chop the cosmos into convenient chunks, however, it perfects no agreement of mind and object. It is my unilateral knowledge without knowing, an intension with no extension, and a disjoined mental state, like the sound of one hand clapping. The applause lacks mutuality, no *consideration* (undertaking, relinquishment, exchange, etc.) signifies its substance. An unquestionable conclusion fails to state a cause of action, and my *immovable belief* (this matter of faith, and *res judicata*) follows purely personal, privileged hypotheses. It is merely a handy *a priori*, my advisory opinion to myself, the fruit of an unripe inquiry, and a demurrable prayer for a fractured form of judgment. Diction without restriction is a moot dispute. True faith transcends any "stake" in the case.

It has no interest in the earthly outcome. My faith *has no standing* in a court of language.[16]

Language is *not* a "veil" of words and syntax, nor a conduit for the True Truth that is draped between the Mind and the Really Real, which might adequately describe perfectly pre-perfected objects getting bounced through menageries of mental mirrors. But language is a luminous catalyst of creativity. Ever since rational choice first carved into the cacophonies of possibility, and beginning with life's most primal percepts, *language* writ large has embodied the evolving tools (the modes of cognition, means of deliberation, and media of expression) that organisms *freely* leverage to *infer* — out of nature's probabilistic *determinations*, and into the infinite iterations of life's transposing redescriptions and attendant *behaviors* — the streaming arrays of perpetually forming and dissolving, aesthetically constructed worlds. Mental activity (mind and consciousness, the intensional, the phenomenal, etc.) is *intrapersonal* language, communication is *interpersonal* language, and *all thinking is linguistic*. It ranges from the autonomic to the ultra-intelligent, and affects every niche of earthly life. From a mosquito's life-or-death, direction-finding

---

16. *See* James, W., *Pragmatism* (Dover, 1995), pp. 17-48 (pragmatic truth and method).

sense of carbon dioxide to the uniquely human search for a good cup of coffee, the apperception of a *realness* being "out there" is *abduced* from open sets of grammatically transposing relations. And if it mattered, these resonating worlds reduce fully into purely *physicalistic* realms, where atomistic, neurological impulses displace each error-termed instant of existence. The objects of thinking, from there being light, hard rocks, and Sherlock Holmes, to the immutable "logical constants," are the continuous weavings of interrelating relations, and a *real* object is *verified* by its virtually invariable redescriptions effecting, in due course, the consensus of fact and our good, stable common sense.

Facts and things comprise endless iterations of actionable hypotheses and settled assimilations, which in themselves constitute derivative, linguistic tools. In leaps and pirouettes of description, various inferences, percepts, and concepts conglomerate out of oscillating processes, from the most incisive and adaptive (creative) to the rigorously logical (critical). Various objects merge through the mind out of migrating meanings. They are not "given," fully baked and "cut at the joints" by the Invisible Angels of Universal Reality, nor by *any* otherworldly, *deus ex machina*, magical metaphor. Interpersonally and intrapersonally, physiologically and metaphysically, *adaptive linguistic behavior* — from preconscious percepts and ostensive grunts, to the finest artwork and revolutionary science — transposes the *neurological* to the *ontological*. Fact follows meaning. The language *is* the concept. And so my talkative mind is *not* some truthful reflection of antecedent "Real" things (real enough, that is, to *describe*) getting "pictured" inside my head (by what means? which map? wherefrom? whose agent?), such that each new picture would be yet *another* distinct object for my uninterrupted cognition (*ad infinitum*), while supposedly producing (*a cappella!*) an "adequate description" (presumably in English) for that "represented thing." Actually, primarily and *creatively*, it's the other way around: *The mind is a function of language.*[17] And the world flips outside in. No heaven-sent intuition explains "universal hotness," let alone, the foundations of Truth and the essence of Reality. Human knowledge does not come so cheap. The cosmos is not that simple. It is the *process of method*, and not the features of somebody's faith, that finds facts, builds Truth, and qualifies knowledge.

---

17. *See* Wittgenstein, L. J., *Philosophical Investigations* (4th Ed.), (Wiley-Blackwell 2009), §§ 19, 75, 109, 119, 135, 139a, 194, 241, 295, 329, 335, 339, 355, 367, 370, 381, 400, 520, 610, 649, 665, 693.

Whenever we seek philosophic understanding, a moment of clarity, or a sandwich, the cognitive irritation elicits further linguistic behavior (inquiry) that tends to attain a correlative cognitive equilibrium (judgment).[18] Cases and controversies produce ranges of changes in the mind (all else is moot). Life's inherent adversity, which *is* given, pits the exigencies of the world against the sums of experience, as deliberative behavior follows psychological imperatives (ethic). When I approach a refined understanding (epistemic), it's like I'm finally seeing a sharper image (aesthetic). The trigonometries of thinking reveal a vibrant dimension for the shaping molecules, objects, and planes of knowledge. Triadic transpositions of an exceedingly problematic, natural environment form enduring, *communicable* realizations and abduce "the Mind." It is the aesthetics of language banging heads with the artistry of existence that sparks-up useful and unwavering ideas (our "practical bearings"), which is the cash value of Truth. So my typically instantaneous intuition, no matter how certain (and beside the point) that things in the cosmos simply *must* have been "hot" before anybody ever talked about it, or felt hot, or thought hot, would

18. Burke, F.T., *Dewey's New Logic*, op. cit., pp. 136-146.

be deduced from non-substantive (illusory), wholly inadmissible premises — it is an inchoate description, a stir-pot of ahistorical figments, and my *categorically voidable* explanation.[19]

. . .

An inference is *not* an essence, and intuitions make flimsy foundations. Within *dimensionless* domains, we more easily envision the primacy of the aesthetic, the fallacy of finality, and "the myth of the given." We have little use for "metaphysical certainty." We are done with the orthodoxic myopia and convergence of all Reason at the end of time. The new millennium would be better baked in contingent paradigms and historical authority, as the melding minds of humanity condense and con-join continuously within billowing cloud chambers of hyperbolically projecting, synaptic molecules, forming the *anthropic* uni-verse. The philosophic is *unfinishable* (except by death), and like obsessed artists, we will "find" only what we have made. We resist repose and

---

19. Calling an illusory explanation an "intuition," or basing knowledge and science upon an indubitable "hunch," is paradise for skeptics and a patently unwarranted shortcut. In practice, it is a *convenience* or apologetic, mythic nonsense.

our souls move. Our knowledge of The Good, Truth, and Beauty is a human-brewed, earthbound ecstasy.

The philosophic is *rough*, also. You can't put a bow on it. Whenever language squares off with existence, philosophy happens. What "exists" is humanity's infinitesimal corner of the cosmos — an organic bubble of Cause and Effect, which is variously called nature, the universe, the world. Beyond this tiny bubble is dimensionless-ness divided by nothingness (whereof one cannot speak). Existence is the sum of *causes*. *Effect* is the sum of language, and linguistic transposition culminating in *behavior* is the first sign and last trace of life on Earth.

The migrations of language are driven by various ranges and admixtures of "hermeneutic continua," such as the absolutely *individual* (my brain being a nonstop network of assimilating predicates and decomposing memories) intermingled with the purely *societal* (people talk, communalize concepts, believe and act conventionally, or not, enculture civilizations, etc.), as consciousness congeals out of galaxies of grammar, stretching from the intuitively *internal* (mental, subjective, personal, and intensional) to the indubitably *external* (physical, objective, communal, and extensional), and along the way, we traverse the visible spectra of *creative* to *critical* modes of contemplation (in the throes of creativity, we ponder critically the "meanings and texts" of language, and upon the secure path of criticism, we create more perfectly adapted worlds). But even with such distinguished distinctions, linguistic meaning is *not* so exalted that only philosophers and lunatics may grasp the illustrious essence of the Really Real. Nor does *meaning* reduce to terms of *analysis* for a stripped-down language of fact-based (*synthetic*) words and judgments.[20] Instead, language and existence resonate expansively, aesthetically, and at the speed of thought, coercing the correlative rhythms of *ameliorative behavior*. Through it all, what we mean *is what we do*. Seeking a truer, newer knowledge is a dangerous road, and the meaning of life evolves inexorably, by natural selection, while we organisms keep scrambling over this biospheric pressure cooker of a blue planet, provoked by an *unbelievably* merciless and fundamentally unfathomable, cosmic resistance.

When the whipsaws of contemplation begin to defy description, words start humming. With language, we relate the objects of each "game" (activity) meaningfully (usefully), and in harmony with the rhythmic

---

20. *See* Quine, W. V., *Two Dogmas of Empiricism*, 60 Philosophical Review, No. 1, pp. 20-43 (1951).

structures of each world. The endless frictions of thinking (language) and nature (existence) effect a knowledge of *predictable* change, and radiant ideas progress from primal predilections to the budding apperception of abstract possibilities. *Life-affirming choice* (rational behavior) ensues, as experience underwrites the aesthetic.[21] That is, *behavior* is "the mirror" of *language*. And in the cognitive heat, the expansive pressures continue. Newly patterned percepts transpose abductively and reconcile rhetorically — they *reconceptualize* like lightning, from the ground up and the middle out. Then maybe, at the far edges of the roiling hodgepodge, from the sumptuous abyss of humanity's incessantly incubating preconsciousness, we sense creative stirrings. *Impulsively*, we move to evoke it. But we don't have "the words." We possess the linguistic means of *experience,* but not yet the means of expression.

"Method-ing" is the fulcrum of language. It acts and reacts at the vertex of "thinking" and "talking" (contemplation and expression), and it is likewise staggeringly complex behavior. Method-ing is the function of *intelligence.* It is rational (i.e. relatable, measurable) and selective (value-based) activity that in due course

---

21. *See* Dewey, J., *Art as Experience* (Perigee, 1980), pp. 36-84 (experience and expression).

reflects and delineates an *aesthetic order*, that empowers human life in this virtually existing (*anthropically inferred*), natural environment. From the primitive to the philosophic, our exceedingly evolved, hard-wired predispositions for *unity* and *order* favor ever more intricate, metaphorical beliefs and behaviors. Humanity's perpetually compounding and dissipating, linguistic transposition structures the *rational* universe (untouched by unspeakable dimensionless-ness) and advances concomitant propensities of action that may prove conducive to life on Earth. Our *adaptive knowledge* is human language in blessed synchrony with the rhythms of the world, from rainy seasons and rotating stars, to an infant's beating heart.

Language enables possibilities for more flourishing lives and nurturing cultures. Self-creation, justice, and social hope are intwined in an unfinishable tapestry.

Traces of the aesthetic are laid bare by the abduction of opulent memories and shattering consequences into refined understandings. We assimilate worldly *effects*, hard-pressed by psychological imperatives. We are pitted and thrown, individually and societally, against an infinitely indifferent, "natural selection" as the autonomous agents of life itself — the *substance of soul* — come what may. Intelligent choice fills a plethora of needs and desires *efficiently* and fashions more *precise* interactions with the environment. We shape *and* adapt to continuous, triadic inferences of a spacio-temporal, uni-versal reality, and the *most* penetrating redescriptions (our truly revolutionary ideas, choices, and beliefs) resound with the resilience and vitality of our most creative behavior. They weave and reveal new patterns throughout the historical and methodological complexities of human activities, and demonstrate the *value* (the meanings and uses) of a finely restrained language. They weigh by words our place in a horrifying, terrifying, incognizable cosmos.

What is "given" is no longer the foundation, essence, and substance of Being, nor some prepackaged diorama of a convergent Reality, where all Truth is out there. Instead, a few billion years ago, life erupted randomly upon the Earth (thinking exists). *We got life.* That's it. The rest is language.

. . .

Then came Existence rising from the ever-revealing relations of potential propositions, comprising unsettleable sets of unveiling vertices — out of integrating inferences into world-whipped waves of abductive abstraction — which *complement* pervasively (hypostatize) correlations of understanding *qua* experience (cause) and conclusions *qua* logical judgment (effect).

In other words, adaptive, grammatic thinking (intrapersonal, linguistic behavior) configures the crunching synapses and integral calculus of the brain, while an atomistic consciousness (from private pains to first philosophy) is molded by the tides, tendencies, and progressions of *transposing redescriptions* (abductively leveraged, ceaseless inferences) that form and modify endless objects, moments, *causes*, etc., as near as my nostrils or *way* far out. The imposing, no matter how easily trounced and forgotten attribute of human intelligence, is that signs, comparisons, words, copies, and images (the indicia of language) don't do much *except* to construe and conjoin *aporistically* further inceptions, perceptions, deceptions, conceptions, and "higher," as it were, judgments. (Otherwise, it'd be like asking that guy in the mirror to keep on shaving, so you can go back to bed.) We are not dazzled by glassy essences, nor appeased by modern myths. We induce meaning from memories, we deduce predictions, and *causation remains the grand hypothesis*. It is simply our grammatically sculpted habit to conceive, if not to believe, *very* fiercely, that we are schmoozing with The Truth itself, that we have finally and inextricably perfected our intercourse with Reality, when we accede in form to what we invariably infer, like saying, "this thing is a stone, stones are hard, therefore, this thing is hard!"

A child of nature (the tyrannical toddler, unimpressed by analysis) would verbalize things less noun-crazy and not so naughty: "I mushed this interesting thingy against my nose, and it felt *just like hardness*. I guess that's *what stone-thingies do*, all the time, so I'll bet if you mushed that *other* stone-thingy against *your* nose, it'll happen again!" Following such sweet conclusions, from unabashedly scientific beginnings, our increasingly incisive invention of knowable names, hard adjectives, and flamboyant "universals" becomes a problem of reifying rhetoric, but *not* a problem of rationalized Reality. And what we've learned since Plato, after so many centuries of plodding, unresolved disputations, is that non-problems have no solution.[22]

The *universality* of Cause and Effect is an immutable rhetorical convenience, rather than some top-down

---

22. Certainly, none that is especially interesting.

epistemological necessity. It is a *mind-altering* adaptation, the life-revealing, divine whisper, the wellspring of the aesthetic, and the keystone of the abductive. It facilitates choice, validates faith, and sustains action. It is logic's analog of real-ness, and along the way, it points to philosophy's *solvable* chicken-or-egg problem: As a matter of fact, Cause does not precede Effect, as much as *effects precede ideas*. I shall explain.

When considered point blank, causation is nothing less than our *ex post facto* substantiation for each and every "real thing" that has yet or might ever engage the mind. It is *the inference-in-transcendence*, a moment's mode of repose, the apparent and seemingly irreducible judgment, which like all cognitions, attains its *meaning* in *conjunction* with prior cognitions and other, unforgotten "signs."[23] The pan-hypostatizing phenomena of causation are abduced as predictable sequences, realistic pictures, and explicable events, and tame the torrents of revealing relations transposing into rational (life-sustaining) beliefs and behaviors. Causation complements the assimilation of distinct "*arguments*" (the measurable percepts of unrelenting change) that signify the infinite actualities

23. Peirce, C. S., *Questions Concerning Certain Faculties*, from *Charles S. Peirce: Selected Writings, op. cit.*, pp. 18-25.

and perpetually morphing molecules of this wild, plunging river of existence.[24]

But every valid conclusion is still another plausible premise. And in our all-too-human impatience to get to "the Final Truth," we indulge fanatically and unsparingly in our hard-nosed belief that "the concept" shall precede the predicate, that "reasons" may exist without reasoning. I call this meta-illusory, non-relating pseudo-function the Bass-Ackwards fallacy. And it's everywhere. It's an inexhaustible source of comedy and

---

24. If you go down by the river, be careful where you stick your foot. Cause and Effect gets transubstantiated *ad nauseam* by nervous "realists," who act like it's *not* profoundly inferential, like it's *not* immediately phenomenal. There can be no fading diagrams in the sand for the apostles of permanence, who cling to the indispensable, peculiar preconditions for any cognizable cause of *intuitively* noncontingent consequences, so that every straight line, for example, shall *invariably* demark two sides! What on Earth? Banality of analysis and kindergarten geometry are not pillars of science, law, philosophy, *or* reality (even if elegantly inscrutable), and they're stuck in this *maddening*, onesie-twosie mind-set. It's like they don't contemplate too much about anything, except the same old stratified dichotomies and delicate differentiations, rudely roused by fashionable buzzwords, ancient lipstick, and sciencey methodologies—*they expound upon nothing*, except with these increasingly threadbare, mindlessly discursive formulations — oh, I am ranting! (We've got to *get out* of this place. I've got to find a *new place* where the kids are hip.)

error. Consequently (in effect?) all language and logic takes this bassackwards half-twist, as each of us cruises along that Möbius strip wrapped through space-time, which is the human mind. And the philosopher or philistine who does not appreciate this — who thinks of *logos* as the omnipotent *a priori*, like a super-arching form and force of nature — will become tucked into a tidy, four-square universe, when all that is out there is pure awesomeness.

There is an implicit and pervasive muddling of Cause and Effect, which takes place when a transcendent, natural language materializes out of the rhetorical art of inventing signs that instill images. Philosophy's inalienable, timeless task of communicating the experience of an astounding realization, of *reproducing* the abduction of a refined understanding by *means* of language — the unceasing exploration for ideas, visions, figures, and forms that may serve to expand the very limits of reflection, elucidation, and analysis — will find within this babbled mishmash of causes its foremost impediment, and perhaps, its richest opportunities.

— CONTEXTUAL —

Creative Obsession is experimental prose. The impetus to complete it emerged from my fascination with the anatomies, constructs, and untapped wealth of aphoristic forms. Following this, I discovered fertile possibilities for piecing a motley mix of blossoming epigrams into finely tuned, philosophical mosaics.

The method underlying *Creative Obsession* has been rigorous.[25] However, a geo-genetic, psycho-synthetic, fully figured, and multithreaded method certainly does *not* engender an integrated, theoretical system. There could arise no epic dialectic, infallible heuristic, or hermetic analysis that might, at the end of the day, show the body of philosophical knowledge as an "organic whole." I've gingerly deferred that life-engulfing, Herculean task (the curse of Sisyphus, some weary practitioners might say), at which the masters of this craft have excelled, of cramming the three-dimensional nature of a comprehensive philosophy into the two-dimensional machinery of a written language,

---

25. Method is the rational aspect of the creative process. It imbues the form as it bares the symmetries of any work — from the ground up! It is the *precursor*, the fertilizer of knowledge, the *quintessence-in-fact* of the human *oeuvre*.

and then struggling against time with the inevitable distortions, not unlike a Renaissance cartographer creating the most perfect, flat map of the Earth.[26]

Instead, these mosaics leave it principally *to the reader* to "connect the dots" into intricate webs. The

---

26. *See* Schopenhauer, A., *The World as Will and Representation* (Dover, 1969), pp. xii-xiii [philosophy, "however comprehensive, must preserve the most perfect unity. If, all the same, it can be split up into parts for the purpose of being communicated, then the connection of these parts must once more be organic, *i.e.*, of such a kind that every part supports the whole just as much as it is supported by the whole; a connection in which no part is first and no part last, in which the whole gains in clearness from every part, and even the smallest part cannot be fully understood until the whole has been first understood. But a book must have a first and a last line, and to this extent will always remain very unlike an organism . . . Consequently, form and matter will here be in contradiction"].

See Ortega y Gasset, J., *Historical Reason* (Norton, 1984), p. 18 ["Philosophy is such a circular reality. The countless ideas of which it consists . . . will possess an order of their own irrespective of our whims; but philosophy lacks an order for beginning and ending. None of its ideas is first, and none last"]; Ortega y Gasset, J., *What is Philosophy?* (Norton, 1964), p. 30 ["In philosophy a straight line is not usually the shortest road. The great philosophic problems yield to conquest . . . by approaching them on a curved path, marching around and around them in concentric circles which become ever tighter and more suggestive"].

book's eclectic segments touch upon diverse moments of actuality, symmetry, validity, and repose. In this pointillistic portrait of a wide-ranging philosophical tradition, the reader must fashion the definitive images, through that indispensable agency of coalescing consciousness and subtle discernment, that fulcrum, vertex, and pivot point of logic, the unheralded *faculty of abduction*.[27] Working it this way can be extremely effective, rhetorically. But of course, it's not the pomp of *any* circumstance. Although I've channeled the ravaged writer and I've played the dogged alchemist, whipping-up billowing crucibles of words and pith, I don't profess about things in particular. So I've tried to keep in mind that there's nothing much more annoying than a persistent poet, or some other instigator, who speaks "out of school." (Which is not to deny that we're all guilty of this embarrassing sin, nor that it's incumbent upon all honest persons — once we find them — to explore with due care and diligence the metes and bounds of the knowledge they may have attained.)

That said, I will venture an opinion — as a journeyman lawyer and a would-be artist, who has dabbled and sometimes waded into philosophy books, on and

---

27. *See* Peirce, C. S. *Philosophical Writings of Peirce*, op. cit., pp. 150-156 (abduction and induction).

off for almost (good grief) 27 years — that academic and peripatetic philosophy have labored under a crisis of cultural inconsequence for the past few centuries, not because the objects of our thinking have been changing faster than we can think about it, but because the *language* (broadly speaking) of philosophy has simply not been up to the task.[28] The philosophers' diligent search for contradiction and error, and their precise, discursive methods of exploration, exposition and review, were prodigiously productive in the 13th century. Following that flowery flourish of the *dialectic cum analytic* fetish, there have been radical, antithetical changes in social institutions and science, and accordingly, in the *grounds* (the beans in the boiling pot) of philosophy. But who can pretend, other than a happy specialist, that there have been correspondingly radical changes in the *methods* of philosophy? An obsolete method is like a black hole. It sucks the light out of anything that gets too close. The syllabi of philosophy are *dissolving* (spawning reams of inbred, eager-beaver semi-science and insular, artless esoterica — angels and pins, all over again), because

---

28. *See* Foucault, M., *Preface to Transgression*, Bouchard, D.F., ed., *Language, Counter-Memory, Practice* (Cornell University Press, 1977), pp. 29-52.

in a civilization forged by machines and information, to grow more obscure is a mark of impotence, if not irrelevance. As we look back, we find troubling indications that *the limits of philosophy* — the breadth of choice and depth of action that it might affect, and the sphere in which human thinking remains clear and distinct — these limits have been shrinking, *they are evaporating*, and in the wake of those surging sciences, perhaps drastically so. This paradoxical contraction and dissolution, as we decipher yet again the inexorable movement of human affairs, is deeply disquieting for doers and teachers who *do* profess that philosophy's ancient covenant remains undisturbed, that it might advance the finer arts of judgment (in worlds where there are only shades of grey) and instill a powerful and profound sense of humanity upon persons, entire nations and cultures. Since the days of Descartes, decorated legions have challenged the burgeoning obfuscation, *brilliant* meteors have showered the dark skies, and still, the dissolution continues.

I don't have radical inclinations, although I've been impressed that philosophy needs radical, innovative methods. At this moment in the history of deliberative thinking, a more portentous and as such, *authentic* question for philosophy (maybe it's not "the first of all questions," but who cares?)[29] is looming and unstoppable — what *new* methods of reflection and exposition, that is, what untried processes at the outer limits of language, might allow us to *transgress* increasingly unto the far frontiers of human intelligence?[30]

Journeymen don't enjoy warm chairs, so I'm a lot less constrained to suggest an appropriately radical requisite for any *effective* method of philosophy, which is that *epochal and transgressive results* entail the correlative development of *monumentally groundbreaking* (mind-blowing) philosophical genres. Seriously. The Third Millennium isn't waiting, and philosophy, if it is to thrive, or at least not turn into stone, must reassert its place as the principal protagonist of the living languages, as a leading actor on the steely edge of the rhetorical arts. Philosophy has played this role before, most radiantly, in its days of vim and glory. But the Delphic riddle, the geometric demonstration, the dialogue, and the tome, like warmed-over metaphors transposing into literal language, have exhausted their once impervious powers to influence the course of civilization. (Essays and monographs would be next.)

---

29. *Compare* Heidegger, M., *An Introduction to Metaphysics* (Anchor Books, 1961), pp. 1-8.
30. *See* Foucault, M., *Preface to Transgression, op. cit.,* pp. 29-52.

When the question concerns the rebirth of philosophic knowledge, of attaining clear and *actionable* ideas at the most inaccessible reaches of rationality and analysis, new figures set into old molds just don't cut it anymore.

I hope you'll pardon my pride of authorship, but I'd like to say what's been on my mind for a long time. *Creative Obsession* is hard to classify, and therefore, it's different. It could be a throwback to pre-Socratic fragments, a more modernistic *pensées*, or an inimitable intimation of some formidable philosophy from a post-polemical, un-universal, and still-too-human future. It's not poetry and it's not drama. There's no comedy, no tragedy, and no novel. It is ironistic, quasi-analytical and semi-conjectural prose, a compounding conglomeration of discriminating redescriptions, and *thoroughly* circumscribed, such that (frills and apologues aside) this was *not* a work of fiction. Nor is it nonfiction. Certainly, it is neither a treatise nor a thesis. It is, at once, argumentative, expository, narrative, *and* theoretical — I wouldn't want to peg that. What I *can* say, with conviction, is that the subject of *Creative Obsession*'s experimental prose is *philosophy*, in every vital sense of the word.

Nietzsche (I resort again to authority) grasped the fundamental need for untried modalities of philosophic elucidation. His most striking work, however, was not his long, schmaltzy allegory, *Thus Spoke Zarathustra*. Following that elaborate study, Nietzsche resumed his presentation by means of expository aphorisms (more or less), demonstrating further his unsurpassed rhetoric, in that Nietzsche's blistering visions were extremely arduous to describe and painstakingly, genuinely original. So it's a sensible hypothesis that a new and potentially earth-bending genre of philosophy might be some kind of mutation, variation, or continuation of fictional and expository aphorisms. As a whole, and in particular, *Creative Obsession* is a sporting trial of this hypothesis, or so it's been turning out.[31] The complementary discreteness and interrelatedness of the book's diverse, aphoristic segments exemplify an extravagantly reduced literary form, the *apomary*.

— BIOGRAPHIC —

Reasonable people could say, after taking stock of *Creative Obsession*, that this apomary is "*complete* [rhetoric], devoid of *any* [fudging] system." As I've suggested, a

---

31. *See* Ortega y Gasset, J., *Historical Reason, op. cit.*, pp 24-25.

measure of criticism along these lines would be astute. Any "system" (any hypostatizing, systemic synthesis) within the apomary is merely the incidental expression of a fleeting, philosophical framework, the rocking cradle of my extracurricular assimilation of the aesthetic (my mind *in communion*), a bootstrapped, immutable mold for a *uni-verse*, and a preconscious ordination (from brainstem to guts) for an unscalable chart of reality. My framework may be as unique as my thumbprint, but I've borrowed, begged, and inherited all the materials, plans, and specifications. As a matter of law, I could have no patentable, philosophical opinions. I've come to understand that anything useful and nonobvious that I might say about Greek thinking is already reflected somewhere in the prior art. Like a lot of people, I keep finding astounding passages in masterful books that remind me of images I've contemplated half-consciously for years. (We need these jaw-dropping revelations. They allow us to believe that our most intimate ruminations have been authentic.) I try to be explicit about the authors who have surely influenced me, whether or not I stumbled across the work before I encountered their resonant echoes. My framework reveals the person I have been, the traditions I respect, and the philosophers to whom I am indebted.

My beginnings as an apomary writer may be typical. I started writing exceptionally bad poetry at a young age. A few years later, I started reading philosophy. After that, nothing too remarkable happened, except that as a law clerk, and thereinafter as a lawyer, I got paid to write as clearly, concisely, and effectively (or as prolifically) as I could. I was born to a loving family, a fine education, zilch for a fortune, and a thick head. When it came to my psychobabble poetry, however, it served to inform my self-understanding, but I knew that it was inferior artwork. I never bothered to save my poetry.

Then, when I was 30, a strange poem leaped boldly and not too awkwardly from the tip of my chopped-up pencil. I had no idea what it was, still I liked it and I kept it. This poem was like one of those sudden, soul-arresting realizations that I often had when I was young — that *everybody* keeps having from time to time — when there flashes through the mind a fragmentary, shimmering new awareness concerning the most acute association of "heavy" ideas, and it produces a brief, "light" and intense feeling of clear understanding, and yet it's almost *impossible* to explain to yourself what the unannounced annunciation could *possibly* mean, or to maintain the intense feeling, and then about ten or twenty seconds later, you can't even remember what the realization was all about; except that this time, *there were words* for it, and somehow, I embraced it. I captured it, I polished it, I polished it some more, and there it was. When that oddball poem was writhing and kicking into existence, I had a visceral feeling, which to my surprise did not diminish over time, that the images it carried were taken from the primal underground and mother earth of my philosophic experience.

Over the next four years, I conjured, juggled, and figured out about twenty of these invasive "un-poems." By then, I had surmised (and how) that these scattered, "metrical compositions of rhyme and rhythm" were *aphorisms*, astonishingly *disparate* aphorisms, and it was unsettling to discern the irreconcilable designs being drawn from the same well, each harkening to the same, confounding books of modern wisdom. Moreover, when various elements were juxtaposed, new areas of meaning and insight would appear. (They started taking on lives of their own!) I began believing that these orienting oracles might come to coalesce — out of my chaotic, creative temperament, no less — an unparalleled, pixelated panoply of (what *is* this?) perspicuous prose and a radically *diverging*, hyperbolic projection of raw reality. Before too long, I got the pesky, clingy, and then unshakable idea that if I could generate enough aphorisms, and if I rendered them into meaningful sequences, that I just might leverage a brazenly literary and exceedingly concise explication of philosophy.

When I was 34, I began a fifteen-month, overseas sabbatical. On that long trip, I explored further the exhilarating, protolinguistic origins of these profoundly dissimilar aphorisms. I unveiled to myself dozens of pristine creations and thousands of promising, nuanced variations, while my travels aroused an abundance of fascinating, wondrous, and maybe-not-so-inarticulable apparitions from the edge of the world. *Perfect Minds* began to materialize on a rusted-out copra boat, during a 26-day excursion to the southernmost islands of Lau. *Scary Planet* came full circle in a rat-infested, fiber-board hotel on the banks of the Mahakam River, about a four-day, putt-putting journey by overcrowded taxi boat, up from Samarinda. *The Last Act* was finished (I had supposed) in an idyllic little garden that I found in an isolated corner of Bali. Also, when I was holed-up at the St. Kilda Coffee Palace, I started giving titles to the aphorisms, which set into motion new layers of rhetorical problems and possibilities.

When I was on the road, I felt like I was in heaven. But that was, I'll be damned, all she wrote. I haven't written an aphorism from scratch in about ten years. This doesn't bother me too much, because my opportunity, as I understood it, was to expound my core repertoire *once*.[32] From the beginning, it's been vexingly obvious that inessential ballast, fill, or repetition could only dilute the work. Since my sabbatical, I've been consumed by my professional and business interests. Every so often, once a year or so (and then increasingly — then unremittingly), I would turn my full attention to the apomary, what the hell, just one more time.

The ordering and re-ordering of the seemingly solid and persistently malleable aphorisms became ridiculously complicated as my collection grew. At one point I had corralled, by my accounting, sixty-three *discrete* compositions. (*Holy cats!*) How many ways

---

32. Not long after expounding these lines, a while back, I traveled in Yemen (a spectacular country) for five weeks, where I excogitated (blasted, carved and chiseled-out) three new aphorisms. Traveling solo takes me to the place where aphorisms come from, although the way I see it, *one apomary, per author, per lifetime* is a defining aspect of the apomary. Apparently, the occasional, supplemental aphorism, if it aligns precisely within the work, should be allowed into the mix.

are there to shuffle a deck of sixty-three cards? (*Lots!*) "Naturally," it became "necessary" (actually, I'd been swiftly swaddled and stringently restricted by the ineluctable logic of an authentic aesthetic) to experiment with a variety of ideas relating to the arrangement of aphorisms, which might expose the most fulsome matrices of meaning and allusion, that is, allusions more sharply evocative of a pervasive *web of hypotheses*, an aporistic *ether of consciousness*, that bedrock and canvas affecting *each* creation, including *this* spiraling portrait, yet another shared vision of philosophic life.[33]

---

33. Twilight! Already? As the decades rolled by and the dots filled-in, I more distinctly observed within myself an order of consciousness that is fundamentally *aporistic*, and modes of understanding that are predominantly *dialectic*. I've been dealing with thoroughly vague, but glistening and starkly lifelike premonitions (there's just no end to it) that in reality, logic *merely* comprises eternally useful, unwavering relations (like fixed, twinkling stars), whereas in fact, logic functions *only* as we have come to express it. It flips me out again, this uninvited, two-strikes, peek-a-boo episteme. And so, in an inexorably temporal uni-verse (a perfectly imagined domain for an *objective*, natural world), the *complementary* effectiveness of dialectic, aporistic, and analytic knowledge — these rationally woven, phenomenal fabrics of realizing reality, radically reduced and reasonably rendered through sweeping

To begin with, what implicit paths of meaning and development could the rudimentary arrangement of these aphorisms conceivably reveal? For example, might cogent and compelling transitions from the "ethical" to the "critical" be identified or refined, and if so, what intricacies of mind or subtleties of description could such movements reflect or engender? Should pieces be grouped thematically, chronologically, by form, mood, etc.? Or sown to the four winds? But then, what untested sequences might better illuminate dynamic sums of ideas, or produce more telling lines of association among certain aphorisms, and what other themes, structures, words, etc. should or shouldn't intervene? There were innumerable conundrums and unceasing resistance. All the while, I had to unravel a lot of mistakes.

---

aesthetics and communal deities, while displacing a probabilistic, mirage-like edifice of rhetorically laden and logically laced, predicating peculiarities — *now con-geals before me*, belatedly, as the crux of the philosophical question, the apomary's *un*-bassackwards ("heliocentric"), respectful variation and subliminal, driving force for all these years — I'm beginning to get it, thanks to my steadfast dog (my scruffy, little Apo), who sits beside me, still the excited pup as once again we are descending a long, steep, bumpy road. I'm just not so sure this banged-up jalopy will make it down there this time. It's getting time to let the dog out, I suppose.

Each change uncorked a ripple effect. Waves of misgivings, stubborn disambiguations, or minute variations to the rhythms and contours of aphorisms were triggered by continuous disturbances in the Order, and vice versa. Scrupulous rearrangements caused several aphorisms to be discarded for failing to "fit" anywhere, only to be resurrected splendidly (or dragged back in) when differing alignments were poked, probed, and tried. Other aphorisms, which had bunched together like organic carrots, were eventually separated or reunited, or split-up for good. This whack-a-mole process of successive approximation kept me busy reworking every wrinkle in sight, repeatedly and relentlessly. Soon enough, an afterword began to amass within the swirling mix (like a luminous, orbiting moon — and after years of flying blind, it was nice to see a few landmarks emerging from the shadows). I was enthralled again, as the work assumed this dazzling, second axis. But throughout the apomary's interminable gestations, I found myself repeatedly kowtowing away and then tiptoeing back to the ever-mushrooming complexities and perplexities appearing before me. Streams of recontextualizing revisions to the otherwise discrete and complete aphorisms were handled with a *delicate* deliberation and *assiduous* appeals to the primal epiphanies (the wistful and duly fading, philosophic authorities of my soul). Meanwhile, this tar baby of an apomary grew more fraught with serendipitous associations and latent meanings, as unchained rhetoric, in pursuit of the unrestrainable aesthetic, honed each and every pixel, line, and image. And the rigor instilled a needed assurance that each exoteric figure and every shiny, compromised aphorism (I loved them all) had to be trashed.

Also, there were many *recurring* difficulties during these drawn-out proceedings — interesting, implacable problems like, which aphorism should go first? I'd been mired in a sweet pickle of mobile metaphors. Then, for the last time, I realized it was finished.

— Viator E. O'Leviter
Oakland, California

Viator E. O'Leviter is the pseudonymous author of *Creative Obsession*. He is a lawyer in private practice, who enjoys a sequestered, literary life.

The apomary is a form of art suited to philosophic elucidation, where the lines between readership and authorship grow increasingly unsettled. The meticulously blended imagery of the *aporistic* work portrays, in this instance, *the itinerant inquirer*, a worldwise mosaic-maker, whose indefinite and dissipating presence portends the nom de plume.

"Viator E. O'Leviter" is good advice in bad Latin. It means to travel lightly, yet passionately, and to "play the hand that's dealt you," as you might, come what may.

Viator (Paul Hunt) was born in Oakland, California, and he grew up in Berkeley during changing times. He is a graduate of Columbia University and the University of San Francisco. He lives in Oakland with his beautiful wife, in an old and comfy home.

www.ingramcontent.com/pod-product-compliance
Lightning Source LLC
Chambersburg PA
CBHW020521120726
47904CB00003B/920